JESSIE'S WEDDING

JESSIE'S WEDDING

•

Kathryn Quick

AVALON BOOKS
NEW YORK

PRINTED IN THE UNITED STATES OF AMERICA
ON ACID-FREE PAPER
BY HADDON CRAFTSMEN, BLOOMSBURG, PENNSYLVANIA

For Mom

Prologue

Jessica O'Brien knew that the next few minutes were going to be among the most important in her life. At least that was what her mom told her right before she handed Jessie the small wicker basket full of spring flowers and whispered the duties of a flower girl into her ear for the hundredth time.

Waiting impatiently to begin after her mom was seated, Jessie dug the toe of one shiny pink leather shoe into the worn red carpeting of the church vestibule and then smoothed the skirt of her pink organdy gown. In a sudden attack of panic, she hiked up the bell-shaped skirt with one hand and looked to see if she had scuffed the shine on her shoe. Satisfied nothing was ruined, she arranged the petals in her basket to what she thought was a prettier combination of pinks, reds, and whites.

Stepping forward, she pushed open the heavy oak doors that led into the church. When the noise made

1

by the door opening caused many of the guests to turn toward the back, she smiled broadly and waved. With a returning smile her mother shooed Jessie back behind the doors and reminded her with hand gestures to stand up straight and walk slow.

Dropping her shoulders, Jessie pursed her lips in response and shut the door. She remembered what she had to do. After all, she was six years old. Hardly a baby anymore.

"Why look at you, honey," her Grandma Ginger said, placing a white-gloved hand on Jessie's small chin and gently lifting her face. "You look like a fairy princess."

Grinning, Jessie forgot her annoyance and spun in a quick circle, a few of the petals in her basket spilling over the edge and fluttering to the ground. "Grandma, do you like my dress?"

"It's almost as beautiful as you are, honey." Jessie's grandmother turned toward a groomsman standing in the vestibule waiting his turn to seat the guests. "Doesn't my granddaughter look just darling?" she asked, taking his arm.

"Absolutely," he replied softly, winking at Jessie. "She's the prettiest flower girl I've ever seen."

Jessie beamed and pushed a wayward lock of blond hair over her shoulder. She walked to the side door to watch the usher escort her grandmother to a seat but just as she got there, the same curl whipped back into her face.

"You look just daarrr-ling," a voice behind her mocked.

Jessie spun on her heels, feeling heat rise across her cheeks. "More darling than you, Jarrett Collins."

"Ring bearers are handsome," Jarrett said, sticking a finger between his neck and the crisp white of his scaled-down tuxedo shirt. He pulled the collar forward, nearly popping the pink bow tie set at his throat. "Even in this itchy stuff."

"It's not itchy. You're just not used to getting dressed up. I dress up all the time. I'm going to be a ballerina, you know," she said, doing a graceful pirouette for emphasis. "And ballerinas always wear pretty things like this."

"Well I'm going to be a baseball player, so maybe I'll wear this down the aisle," Jarrett said, a smile lighting his face. He opened the center button of the shirt and revealed a shirt emblazoned with a blue and orange New York Mets logo.

Jessie gasped in horror. "Why are you wearing that?"

He reached inside the pink cummerbund around his waist and pulled out a handful of baseball cards. "Because I'm going to drop these as I go down the aisle just like you're going to drop those flowers."

Putting a hand to her waist, Jessie gave him a cocked hip pose. "You better not."

Jarrett took a step forward. "Why not?"

"Because."

"Because why?"

Jessie put down the basket and crossed her arms in front of her chest defiantly. "Because this is MY wedding and no one's gonna ruin it by doing something stupid like that, that's why."

"It's not your wedding."

"Is so."

"Is not."

"Is so. My Aunt Kim said she was gonna share it with me," Jessie said, lifting her chin incontestably.

Momentarily defeated, Jarrett wrinkled up his nose.

"So what if it is your wedding then. Who's gonna stop me?" he said, stepping even closer to her.

Toe to toe with him now, Jessie was not about to back down. "Me, that's who."

"Oh yeah? Well no stinky girl can stop the great Jarrett from doing anything he wants to," he said, before yanking once more on her hair and retreating to the other side of the small vestibule. With an occasional smug glance in Jessie's direction, he showed the collection of baseball cards he had brought with him to one of the ushers.

Jessie stamped her foot and tossed the lock of golden hair back over her shoulder. Wasn't it just like a boy to bring toys to a wedding? She let out a long sigh of superiority and narrowed her eyes at him. Boys simply had no idea how important weddings were. Okay, maybe it wasn't really her wedding, but it wasn't just any wedding. It was her favorite aunt's wedding, and that made it more than special.

She picked the basket up and shot Jarrett a warning look. "You better put those cards away. We're going to start soon."

In response, Jarrett put two of the cards in his mouth and walked back to her. Circling around her, he flapped his arms and pretended to be a duck.

Jessie's blue eyes darkened to the color of thunderclouds. "If you do anything to wreck this wedding, I'll . . ."

Jarrett removed the cards from his mouth and waved them in front of her face. "What can you do? You're just a girl."

Jessie didn't hesitate. She ripped one of the cards from his hand and shoved it inside her basket beneath the flowers. "That's what I'm going to do."

"Hey! No fair. Give it back," Jarrett protested, lunging at her.

"Not until the wedding is over," Jessie responded, taking a step to the side and lifting her chin in triumph as Jarrett flew past her. "And if you do anything else to me . . ." She stopped. A devilish smile curled her pert lips before she turned it into a glower. "I'll rip the card up into a thousand pieces and throw it in the aisle along with the flowers."

"Hey! You better not. It's a very valuable card." Jarrett's face took on a rancor of its own. "If you wreck it, you'll have to pay for it."

"Will not," Jessie said emphatically.

"Will too."

"Will not."

Jarrett narrowed his eyes. "Will too. It's worth twenty dollars, and I can't just go get another one. They don't make them anymore."

"Then you shouldn't have brought it here."

"Give it back," he demanded, grabbing again for the basket but missing as Jessie deftly moved it out of the way once more.

"You have to earn it back," she said, a teasing tone settling into her voice.

Jarrett furrowed his brow. "How?"

"By behaving like a gentleman," Jessie challenged, holding the basket behind her with both hands. She grinned broadly. "I just bet you can't do it. I bet I get to keep the card forever."

Jarrett moved toward her again, but as if on cue, the double doors opened, causing both children to stop dead in their tracks. One of the ushers poked his head inside. "Everyone ready?" He swung the doors open wide, letting the rumbling music of the organ in the balcony drift inside. "It's time. Here we go."

The strains of the wedding march made Jarrett suddenly acquire proper wedding stiffness. He moved to Jessie's side as the bridesmaids took their places in the lineup.

Inching toward the door, Jessie felt Jarrett squeeze her elbow. Balancing the ornate satin pillow holding the rings in one hand and shaking his finger in her face with the other, he made sure the expression on his face told Jessie that he was not happy. "Nothing better happen to that card," he warned her with a faint touch of hysteria in his whispered voice.

"Nothing will," she insisted, moving the basket to her other arm for good measure. "Unless you mess up."

Beaten, Jarrett snorted quietly. "Okay, but that card better not smell all flowery when I get it back or it won't be worth as much in a trade."

Before Jessie could answer him, someone whispered "Go" and gave her and Jarrett a nudge, gently propelling them into the church. There, amid secret whispers and approving smiles, Jessie and Jarrett stepped onto the white runner in the center aisle and, in perfect precision, began the long walk to the altar. In a no-nonsense fashion, they submitted to the flash of camera bulbs and the oohs and ahs of relatives as though they had been paired for this moment by the angels in heaven.

Halfway down the aisle, Jarrett turned, looked at Jessie, and grinned. At that instant, somehow, Jessie knew that one day she was going walk down the aisle with him again. She didn't know how she knew it or why she knew it. She just did.

And maybe, just maybe, somewhere along the way, he was going to get his baseball card back too.

Chapter One

"If those clowns with the rescue squad don't arrive soon, that baby is going to be old enough to drive himself here!"

Dr. Jarrett Collins paced the black-and-white checkered tile floor of Midwest Medical's emergency room and looked at his watch for the fifth time. He cocked his head left, his ears straining to pick up the sound of the siren signaling the arrival of the ambulance.

"Relax, Dr. Collins," a sandy-haired male nurse rolling a wheelchair to the doorway said in response. "You'd think this was your first delivery."

Jarrett strode to the attendant. "What's your name?"

"Ed." The reply faded to a hushed stillness.

"Well, Ed," Jarrett said, squeezing cool annoyance into both words. "This might not be my first delivery, but it's just as important. Each one is." His tone silenced the muttering voices of nurses within earshot. He turned his head briefly to them before continuing.

"You never know what can happen during childbirth, so you had better be ready for anything. And we ARE ready, aren't we, Ed?"

The orderly nodded woodenly and ducked into an empty examining room as the whispers began again.

"A little testy today, aren't we, Dr. Collins?" Ann Ryan, an attractive dark-haired nurse behind the receiving desk, asked with raised eyebrows. "Did we get up on the wrong side of bed?"

Jarrett looked up from his watch. "No, and . . ." The faint whine of an approaching siren caught his attention, and he cocked his thumb in the direction of the parking lot. "Saved by the siren, Ann." He glanced at his watch again. "While I'm in delivery, ask those clowns in the ambulance why it took them thirty minutes to get a woman in premature labor here from the parking deck of a shopping mall only three miles away."

He barely had time to turn around and start toward the emergency entrance when the double doors swished open. His eyes widened and he watched, speechless, as two circus clowns in full makeup burst inside. They were pushing a gurney carrying a very pregnant and very unhappy woman.

"I want this baby out NOW!" she screamed, grabbing onto the arm of the clown in the bright hot pink and lime green striped coat. He grimaced as she squeezed hard on the soft area just below his elbow. "Make the pain stop or this one dies!" She yanked on the rainbow print tie she was gripping in her other hand for emphasis.

The tie was attached to another clown in an oversized yellow trench coat who was trying to help steer the stretcher with one hand and pry the woman's fingers from around his necktie with the other. When he finally did snap it free, he jerked backward, smashing his hip against the wall and setting off a loud blast from the rubber horn attached to his belt. A burst of laughter erupted from the staff working at the nurses' station.

As the unlikely trio came at him in a dead run, Jarrett put out his hands to stop them. "What is going on here?"

Ann stepped from behind the desk, a smug look dancing across her face just as the gurney slammed into Jarrett's outstretched hands and bumped to a stop an inch from his right foot. "Why Doctor Collins, I do believe it's the clowns you were expecting with your maternity patient."

Also dressed in full clown makeup, Jessie O'Brien walked into the emergency room just as the exasperated maternity patient and the convoy of ER staffers and paramedics surrounding her headed into one of the free examining rooms.

"What on earth are you doing here, and in that get-up?" Ann called out, as she saw Jessie pull the curly red nylon wig from her head. "When did you get back?"

Jessie ran her fingers through her thick blond hair. "Yesterday. You know I'd never miss the fund-raiser for the squad. Like my new outfit?" she asked, tugging on the bright purple pants she was wearing. She pointed to a box of tissues on a file cabinet behind the desk. "Hand me some of those, please."

Ann tossed her the box. "How's your grand-mother?"

"Better, thanks. It was just a mild stroke," Jessie said, making a valiant attempt to remove the white face paint from her cheeks. "No paralysis, thank heavens. But the doctor in Minneapolis did tell her that she has to slow down a bit."

"No more mule riding into the Grand Canyon then?"

"That's right. And no more skydiving. She's been grounded."

Ann leaned an elbow onto the counter. "How does she come up with these adventures at her age?"

"I have no idea. But Grandma Ginger has always been the anomaly in the family. O'Brien women tend to be a lot more cautious when dealing with the unknown."

Ann gave her a level look and handed the chart she was working on to another nurse who slid it on back into its place in the file. "It's in the genes, then."

"What's in the genes?"

"You missed a spot with the tissue," Ann replied, pointing to Jessie's forehead. "This propensity you have to hold back is a family thing. I thought you were just being careful."

"Hold back on what?" Jessie asked quickly.

"I wasn't the one who refused to go out with that nice pharmaceutical salesman who stopped in here last month."

"I don't date the proverbial traveling salesmen."

"Then what about the teacher you met when you took that course at Community College? What was his name anyway?"

"Tony. And he had just broken up with his girl-friend."

Jessie tossed a tissue into the wastebasket. "He was a rebounder. In a few weeks he'd probably have gotten back together with her, and then where would I have been?"

Ann picked up a chart and began to write. "What

"They finally hired a new chief of Emergency Medicine, and he's creating quite a stir around here, to say the least."

"Really? Keep going."

"He's tall, drop-dead gorgeous, and, I hear, newly single."

"Sounds promising," Jessie said, interested. "Is he here now?" She looked around but saw only familiar faces.

"He's in with the maternity case you just brought in." Ann leaned closer and lowered her voice. "I'm telling you, this guy is causing more excitement than the time Mayor McDaniels ran off with the redheaded waitress from the Bagel Barn. If I wasn't married, I think I'd be more than tempted by that smile of his to throw my hat into the ring."

Jessie arched an eyebrow. "He must be something to entice *you*."

"This town may be called Tempest, but you know as well as I do that Mundane would be more appropriate. That kind of six-foot, hunky appeal doesn't come along every day and set up housekeeping in a place like this. Mark my words: either he's in the witness protection program, or he's running from a broken heart."

"Maybe you're jumping to conclusions."

"Don't think so. Why else would someone like that choose to come to an ordinary, quiet town in the middle of nowhere when he had the excitement of living in the city that never sleeps?" Ann shrugged. "Heartbroken or hiding, he's fair game around here."

"Step back and get out of my way, ladies; I'm about to mark my territory," Peggy Clark, another emergency room nurse, interrupted as she walked by, snap-

about the hockey player you ran into at the i
last winter?"

"He was traded to the New Jersey Devils, \
made him a GUP."

Ann looked up. "Made him a what?"

"A GUP. A Geographically Undesirable Pers
Someone further away than the thirty-minute-drivir
distance rule." Involuntarily her thoughts began \
drift back, reminding her of a time when she woul\
have driven thirty days straight to try to make a long
distance relationship work.

"Speaking of time frames, we all thought Matt was
going to have to deliver that baby in the ambulance,"
Ann said.

Jessie set the tissue box on the counter and jammed
the used ones into her coat pocket. "Not while I'm
driving. You know I always get them here on time."
She turned back to the desk and signed some papers
before continuing. "So, anything new happen around
here since I've been gone?"

"Dr. Chadwick finally retired."

Jessie's mouth dropped. "You're kidding. He's been
threatening that for years."

"Well, he finally up and did it. Took down his shin-
gle and headed for Florida," Ann replied.

"What will Tempest do for a pediatrician now?"

Ann shrugged. "Use Family Practice, I guess."

Jessie leaned forward onto her elbows. "I suppose
that was the extent of the excitement."

Ann looked at one of the other nurses and they both
grinned broadly. "Not exactly!" they said in unison.

"It's only been a week," Jessie countered. "What
could have possibly happened to make you two look
like cats with mouthfuls of canaries?"

Ann raised and lowered her eyebrows suggestively.

ping on latex gloves. "You know it's only a matter of time before the man's mine."

"Ever-ready Peggy," Jessie and Ann said in unison. Peggy acknowledged the comment with a wrinkle of her nose and a very unladylike dust-off gesture just before disappearing into the examining room.

"Now there's a woman who knows what she wants," Jessie said.

Ann chuckled. "And from what I hear, she wants everyone."

Jessie rolled her eyes. "If Peggy has claimed the good doctor, the man is doomed." She was about to say more when she saw the clown in the green and pink pants come out of the examining room. "Matt, how's the mother and baby?" She walked toward him while waving good-bye to the nurses at the station.

"The baby's not cooperating, so mama might need a C-section. Her OB's tied up with an emergency across town and can't get here for a couple hours, but he's in contact by phone."

"No wonder she wailed louder than the siren on the way over here." Jessie shifted and looked over Matt's shoulder, hoping to catch a glimpse of the woman through the window next to the examining room door. But the trauma team still surrounding her blocked Jessie's view. "Who'll do it?"

"Baker's covering maternity and Dr. Collins will assist."

Jessie froze. The name immediately threw her mind into reverse and shot her flashes of the bottle-green eyes and the dangerous smile that still managed to creep into her dreams.

"Did you say a Dr. Collins was assisting?" she asked, shifting to get a better view of the inside of the examining room through the window. When she did, her gaze froze on a tall, powerfully built figure who appeared to be in total control. She watched him cross to the other side of the stretcher, his walk bringing back a familiarity that nearly stopped her breath.

"Yeah, Collins. The new doctor from the big city." Matt leaned his hip against one of the waiting room chairs. "Oh, that's right, you don't know. He came on board last week. I don't have any specifics, but the word is, he's pretty good."

Jessie hesitated. Collins. Doctor. From the east. "Naaa," she muttered, shaking her head. "Couldn't be him."

Matt straightened. "Couldn't be who?"

Jessie fought for control of her senses. Her imagination was running wild now as more images raced rapid-fire through her mind, putting the appealing green eyes and dazzling smile she thought about earlier onto the face of the man whose back was still toward her. Her heart thumped with anticipation and then with uneasiness as the picture focused inside her mind.

"I used to know someone by that name who wanted to be a doctor," she replied, pushing the images to the back of her mind. "But that was a long time ago. We've since lost touch." She managed a weak smile. "Which one is this Dr. Collins?"

"He's the one next to Peggy."

Jessie saw the tall figure in hospital scrubs turn, and, shedding his gloves, head for the door. In another second the door opened, a moment more and they were face to face.

He removed the white paper mask from across his nose and mouth and did a quick double take. He leaned closer, peering past the smudges of makeup still remaining on her face. "Jessie? Jessie O'Brien? Is it you under all that gunk?" He cupped her chin with his hand and rubbed what was left of the white makeup from her right cheek with his thumb.

Jessie felt warm and very aware of his touch. She was so surprised by the sensation that she hardly had time to compose herself.

"Jessie. It is you." His fingers lingered for a moment more on her face before he dropped his hand to his side.

His voice greeted her with warm pleasure, the familiarity of its tone vibrating through her as her lips parted in a silent breath of astonishment. "Jarrett," she managed to squeak out, feeling the heat growing on her neck and face. "It's been a while. How have you been?" Her gaze went automatically to his eyes as they always had in the past. They were more distracting than she remembered; a deeper green and more magnetic.

Matt looked at them. "You two know each other?"

All Jessie could do was nod, her round-eyed gaze glued to Jarrett's face. The half-smile that hovered around his lips made every emotion she ever felt for him come together from the past and slam headlong into the present. She saw something flicker over Jarrett's expression when he realized she wasn't responding.

"Yes. We're old friends," he said.

Matt turned to Jessie. "Then this is the guy you started telling me about a few minutes ago."

"I hope you were kind, Jess," Jarrett said, grin widening.

Jessie shook her head with a guilty start, like a little girl getting caught red-handed in a lie. "All I said was that I thought I might know the new addition to the staff."

"And it turns out you do." Jarrett's straightforward answer did not leave any room for doubts.

Matt took up the conversation, and Jessie watched as Jarrett crossed his arms over his broad chest and leaned against the wall. She noticed he had much larger hands than she remembered, and his shoulders were much more massive. But of course they would be. He was a man now, in his thirties, a learned professional with a future firmly set in success.

She studied him, unhurriedly, feature by feature, noticing as she did how the years had changed the boy she once knew so well. The shaggy blond hair she loved to run her fingers through had darkened to gold and had given way to a careful style that added an air of distinction to his handsome face. When he laughed in response to something Matt said, his smile fanned tiny, attractive lines out of the corners of his eyes and displayed a line of straight white teeth. There was so much potent male charm in the way he looked that she had to command herself to breathe.

He was in his twenties the last time she saw him lean against a wall like this. He was going off to medical school, and she thought that he was going to ask her to marry him before he left. Instead he had looked into her eyes and said, "But I'll always love you, Jess. And if you ever need me . . ." Then he stopped speaking and stood there, looking at her, waiting.

She'd merely nodded and shut the door on him. She hadn't been able to think of one sensible thing to say. Through the curtains at the front window she had watched him leave, unable to sort through the jumble of feelings that clogged her heart to find the words that would make him stay or take her with him.

For years she clung to the hope that somehow he would come back for her. But he hadn't, and eventually she had admitted to herself that he never would. She was forced to close the book on her childhood fantasy of marrying Jarrett Collins and grow up fast. Now she didn't need anyone. She had made it all on her own.

"I really have to go . . . Doctor." Jessie found herself having trouble trying to get out his title. How was she supposed to relate to him as a professional when what she was feeling at the moment was anything but? If she thought she had gotten over Jarrett Collins years before, seeing him now made her realize she hadn't even been close to it. "And so do you. Your patient is ready." She gestured to the woman being wheeled by them.

"Hey," the mother-to-be called out when she saw Jessie. "Take care of 'handsome' there for me. He sure knows what he's doing. I feel great now." The woman yawned. "I hope I don't sleep through the birth."

Jarrett patted her shoulder. "I won't let you. I promise."

"I see you've made another conquest, Dr. Collins," Peggy said, helping guide the stretcher toward the elevator.

Jarrett laughed. It was a rich chuckle that seemed to reach out to Jessie and caress her with its warmth. "Only since the sedative kicked in. Before that I was on the hit list right after the clown."

Peggy smiled and brushed a strand of bright red hair from her eyes with one hand. "Doctor, you'd be first on my list," she called back as she walked away.

Jessie noticed Jarrett dip his head and raise an eyebrow. She briefly wondered if the comment was making him nervous or eager. She took a deep breath and adjusted her expression. "I really do have to go, Jarrett."

"And I have a promise to keep."

"Gonna do that C-section?" Matt asked, turning to leave.

Jarrett lightly touched Jessie's elbow, urging her to walk with him as he spoke. "First, we're going to try to turn the baby. Hopefully that will put him in the right position and nature will take its course. The mother's doing fine and there's not really a risk to the baby if we wait a little longer. I'd rather not have to go in and get the little guy if I can avoid it," he said smoothly.

"Good luck," Matt said as he took a right turn at the next hallway and disappeared in the direction of the coffee shop.

"You do look wonderful, Jessie." Jarrett said, stopping at the elevator and pressing the up button. Jessie didn't reply.

While he waited for the car, he searched her face for traces of the girl he had left so many years earlier. But even with streaks of silly white clown makeup still evident across her cheeks, he could see that a beautiful woman had replaced that girl.

He tipped his head curiously at her. "A penny for your thoughts." He watched her cheeks color through the makeup, but noticed she firmly held his gaze.

She shook her head. "I don't understand."

"I take it you're not glad to see me?"

"Yes, of course I am. It's just that—" She broke off as the elevator doors opened.

"It's just what?" The elevator doors closed and left without him.

"Don't you have to get up to maternity?"

"She needs to get prepped. I can catch the next car."

Jessie looked him straight in the eye. "Didn't it occur to you that I might still be here in Tempest and you might run into me some day?" She tried to sound composed, but her voice quavered.

"Yes."

She flinched away from the admission and pressed the elevator call button. "The last time I talked to you, you were going away and it was obvious I wasn't invited to come along."

"I made a mistake. I was wrong to walk away from what we had together."

Stunned, Jessie blurted out the words she had been practicing for years. "Whatever we had, or whatever we thought we had, has been over for quite a while. This isn't the time or the place for a discussion on the past. I'm sorry."

"For what?" He matched her grave tone. "I'm the one who left, remember?"

"Yes you did." For a while silence hung in the air between them like a sword waiting to fall and Jessie made no immediate attempt to change it.

"Is it really important why I'm here?" Jarrett finally asked.

"To me it is."

"Okay, then." He reached out and traced the curve of her cheek with his forefinger. "I know I have no right to say this, but I came back for you."

Jessie's eyes widened. She could find nothing to say as the elevator doors closed and took Jarrett away. Pleasure and misgiving entwined themselves around her heart until the edges of each blurred and she could not tell where one emotion ended and the other began.

He said he had come back for her. It was the last thing on earth she ever expected him to say.

Chapter Two

Full circle. Closure. All the stuff Cosmopolitan articles on rejection and recovery quoted. That's what Jarrett's appearance in Wisconsin meant, Jessie thought as she peeled off the clown costume and tossed it aimlessly onto her bed.

Still reeling from seeing him, she turned on the shower, stepped into the stall, and began washing off the theater makeup, fully expecting the tension to melt away as it always did under a good, hot shower. But it was not meant to be. Images of the times she and Jarrett had together drifted back into her thoughts. As she scrubbed her skin with a thick blue washcloth, through the scented shower gel that smelled like morning rain, she thought she could still recall the aroma of his aftershave.

Enough, she commanded her unruly mind. She turned off the water and jerked the towel from its holder. Quickly she dried herself and wrapped her hair into a towel. She wrapped another around her body and reminded herself that she had read Jarrett all wrong once and it had nearly destroyed her. It would be disastrous to do that again.

Pulling open the bathroom door, she stepped out onto her bedroom rug and walked to the bed. She sat down and reached for the telephone. From memory, she dialed the number.

"Hi, Carrie, is Matt back yet? Thanks." She tapped her fingers on the oak tabletop of the nightstand while she waited for his familiar voice. "Hi, it's me. Hear anything?" She nodded, listening to his response. "No, I have to finish some of the work I brought home from the office first." She paused. "I was hoping we raised enough money to get halfway to our goal."

A loud knock on the apartment door made Jessie look up. "Just a minute," she called. "Gotta go, someone's at the door. Call me when you get the final tally. Bye Matt." She hung up the receiver. "Coming," she called out again in response to another knock, louder this time. Grabbing a blue cotton shift, she peeled off both towels and quickly dressed before raking her fingers through her wet hair and walking to the front door. "Who is it?"

"Three guesses."

She only needed one. "Jarrett?"

"Right the first time," he told her.

She hesitated for a moment before pulling off the security chain. She yanked open the door and stared at him as, grinning, he took a long, lazy look at her.

He reached out and lightly touched her cheek before running the tip of his index finger along her jawline. "I like you better without the clown makeup."

Jessie blinked and wondered if he were just a figment of the same overactive imagination that had possessed her in the shower. "What are you doing here?"

"For now, standing on your porch. Can I come in?"

"I guess." She stepped back and he walked inside. Her imagination might have been working overtime a little while ago, but even on high it never once concocted someone who looked this good. Or smelled this good either, she thought, as he passed her and stood next to the overstuffed armchair near the window. She hooked her wet hair behind her ears and closed the door. "You should have told me you'd be coming over."

He looked around the apartment. "Why, are you expecting someone?" There was a trace of laughter in his voice. "Better change your outfit if you are."

Jessie glared back at him, hoping the heat she felt rise in her chest did not show on her cheeks. "I'm not, although it's none of your business."

He chuckled. "Jess, you're going to have to be a bit more convincing if you intend to be sarcastic. Maybe if you crossed your arms and dipped your head a little."

Jessie was not amused. "If nothing else, you have nerve."

"I prefer the word, confidence. Doctors need confidence when they make important decisions."

"Well, Doctor, whatever decision you've made, I assure you, it's the wrong one in this case." She walked back to the door and put her hand on the knob.

"I'm sorry. I can't accept that. I've made it a practice to never second-guess myself once I've decided on a course of action." In a fluid motion, he sat down on the earth-toned chair opposite the sofa in her living room.

"I think you may need a second opinion this time."

Jessie moved from the door to sit down opposite him, and immediately knew she had made a mistake. From the time she had opened the door to find him standing on her stoop, she had felt shaky. Being this near to him made the feeling worse. She couldn't look at him without thinking how the years had molded the boyish lines of his face into handsome angles. When he reached over and took her hand she felt a momentary jolt. The warmth of his touch felt too good. She pulled herself away. "Did you follow me home?"

Jarrett stretched his arm across the back of the chair. "Nope. I was at the hospital until about an hour ago."

It took a tremendous amount of will to pull her gaze from his incredible mouth. When she succeeded, it was only to become lost in the striking golden glint in the green of his eyes. "How did you know where I live?" she managed to somehow get out.

"I called and asked Matt." Jarrett unfolded himself from the chair and stood up. "I assured him that we were old friends, and he gave me your address."

"He shouldn't have without my permission."

"Ann told me that you worked at the hospital. That makes us co-workers."

"I don't work on the floors. I was only in the ER because of the squad call." She stared into his eyes, willing herself to see hardness, but found only a warmth that drew her deeper into the fire. "Is there a reason you tracked me down?" she asked.

"Because I'm hungry," he said. His smile flashed. "How about you finish getting dressed and I'll take you to dinner?"

"I don't think that's a very good idea."

"Why?"

She looked down and fumbled with a button on her

shift. "Because I'm not sure I want you in my life again."

"A brutally honest answer," he said.

She looked away from his face with its hopeful smile. "I just want to avoid making the same mistake I made as a teenager."

"Older and wiser?"

Jessie nodded.

"I suspected that." He swallowed hard. "Please. Get dressed, Jess. We'll have dinner for old times' sake. And then," he continued smoothly, "If you want, I'll get out of your way."

Jessie's expression tightened. As he had in the past, he was dangling his confidence in front of her like bait hoping she would bite. She pulled free and strode to the door. "I don't think so."

As she reached for the doorknob he touched her hand. It was a light gentle touch, yet forceful enough to immobilize her. She turned to face him, her mouth beginning to form the angry words that would unleash the years of loneliness she felt. But he lifted her hand to his lips and kissed it gently, shattering those words into a million pieces inside her head.

"Please, Jessie. It's only dinner."

She stopped, reeling from the chaos that was raging inside her. Part of her wanted to beat her fists against his chest for hurting her and then coming back as though nothing had happened. But part of her wanted to fall into his arms, lay her head against that broad chest, and feel his fingers stroke her hair.

"I will be having dinner, but it will be alone," she finally said, pulling her hand free again. She yanked open the front door and pointed outside. "Good night, Jarrett."

Defeated, he said nothing more. As soon as he

stepped outside, Jessie shut the door and headed for her bedroom.

She dressed slowly, giving him plenty of time to leave. Leaving on the blue cotton shift, she dried her hair and pulled it into a ponytail with a lacy band. At the sink in the bathroom, she picked up the mascara from her makeup case and began to brush a little over the tips of her lashes.

But as she worked, a fragrance teased her nostrils. Curious, she brought her fingertips to her nose. A scent clung to her skin—his scent—a spicy hint of musk cologne mixed with the essence of the man, his skin, his breath. Dropping the mascara, she turned the water on full force. She lathered her hands with scented soap to free herself of the memories. Then, drying her hands carefully, she lifted her chin in triumph.

In the living room she stared at the imprint of his body in the rumpled Indian-print afghan that had been thrown over the chair in which he sat. She walked to it and smoothed the blanket. Erase any sign of him, she thought. Erase it just like she had before.

For a moment, she stood alone in the room, emotions warring inside her. Years ago, when he first walked away from her, she had been afraid he would never come back. Much later, when she finally faced the pain and buried it, she was afraid that someday he would. And now that he had she had no idea what she was supposed to do about it. He wasn't the boy she fell in love with as a teenager, she could tell that. She only hoped he was beginning to realize that she wasn't the same girl.

Picking up her leather bag, she flicked on the porch light and stepped out into the night. Inhaling deeply, she cleared herself of as much of him as she could and hurried to her car. Just as she lifted the car key to the ignition, the door on the passenger side swung open. A tall, lean figure slid into the seat beside her.

Catching her breath, Jessie stared at the face lit by the dome light. Jarrett smiled back at her. The evening breeze had rumpled his neat hair, and a lock had fallen rebelliously over his forehead. She resisted the urge to brush it back into place.

"You should lock your car. I could have been a mugger."

"You still could be."

"An invitation?"

"A warning that I'm on to you."

"I'll take it under advisement." He settled in and buckled the seatbelt. "I called the service to see how the new mother and her baby were doing," he said, pulling the door shut.

"Jarrett, did you hear anything I said earlier?"

"Some." His eyes held hers. "Don't you want to know how they are?"

She hesitatingly returned his devastating smile. "Of course I do. Did you have to do the section?"

"No." He angled his body toward her. "It was great, Jess. Dr. Baker was about to give up, but I told him I wanted to try one more time to turn the baby. He kept one eye on the fetal monitor and one eye on the mother's blood pressure while I explained to her what I was about to do. Then I told her to take a deep breath and hang on." He spoke in a tone filled with awe and excitement. "And this time, when I tried to spin him, the little guy slid right into position. A few minutes later, he was in his mother's arms."

Jessie could see the fulfillment light his eyes. "You love it, don't you?"

"I can't imagine doing anything else." He said the words with the certainty of a man who could never be satisfied with only a dream. "And by the way, the parents are going to name the baby after both of us. He's going to be called Collin Jesse."

An involuntary smile curled Jessie's lips. "He is?"

"So they say." He gestured to the keys in her hand. "Buckle up and let's go. I'm starving." As Jessie numbly lifted the keys to the ignition and started the car, he eased himself back into the blue velour seat. "I told the hospital we'd be at Casey's in case I was needed. Is that all right with you?"

"I suppose you won't be taking no for an answer."

"At least not about dinner."

Jessie sighed. "I really don't understand any of this."

Jarrett reached over and squeezed her hand. "Dinner first, then explanations."

As Jessie cut her steak into square pieces, she could feel Jarrett watching her every move.

"Are you planning on eating any of that?" he asked, reaching over and snatching a french fry from her plate.

Glancing up, Jessie saw that his eyes had darkened to smoky jade in the soft candlelight. His hair looked thick and touchable. In short, he looked great. Too great. She needed a diversion. As she arranged the meat on her plate into a neat, geometric pattern, she focused on how he looked at a much younger age; sixteen maybe, or better yet, twelve.

He had been all ears with a short crop of hair sticking out from beneath a New York Mets baseball cap. His arms seemed too long back then, gangly with undeveloped sinew and calloused hands from the long

hours they spent wrapped around a baseball bat trying
to hit a curve ball in the batting cages.

But the image didn't last long enough. All traces of
the boy were long gone. With his white sleeves rolled
up to his elbows, he displayed the rock-solid hard
muscle of a man. Soft brown hair dusted his forearms,
and his hands were slender with the graceful, long
fingers she'd expect of a doctor.

He reached for another fry and when he sat back,
his knee brushed her leg under the table. A high volt-
age tingle zipped down her spine. She sat straight up,
moved her legs as close to her chair as she could, and
took a bite of the steak, chewing it with intense concentration. At this moment she felt like she was a teenager again—out of control, twisted into knots, her
heart pounding like thunder—and she didn't like it one
bit.

"This is a nice place," he said, watching her, waiting
for her to say something.

"I suppose you're used to fancier restaurants."

"Not really, there's just more of them concentrated
in a small area back east." She saw his eyes blaze with
sudden memory as he continued. "Remember when
you came to Jersey to visit and I took you to that little
restaurant in New York near Rockefeller Center? It
was the—"

"Don't. I don't want to talk about the past right
now." Of course she remembered it. All the tables had
light blue linen tablecloths and wildflowers in crystal
vases. The floor was real oak and all through dinner
they had played touching games under the table with
their feet.

"Okay, then let's talk about now. I know you volunteer with the rescue squad. What do you do at the
hospital?"

She glanced up at a passing waitress carrying a tray of dishes. "I'm in the billing office in the business wing," she said, fighting to stabilize the wall she had put between them that was quickly crumbling. "I'm in credit and collections."

"Ah, the hard-nosed voice of the past-due bills."

"I try to be."

"Quite a departure from the little girl who wanted to be a ballerina."

"Well, you were going to be a baseball player." The words slipped from her mouth.

Jarrett looked away, studying the print on the tablecloth. "Things change."

"You used to send me all the clippings from the newspaper about your high school team. I remember you won the state batting title by getting four hits in the last game of the season."

"Won it by only two percentage points. But I didn't beat you in the batting cage that summer when you came to visit your Aunt Judy. When we went out to hit you kinda distracted me."

"How?"

"You had on a Mets tee shirt and the tightest pair of pants I had ever seen, and I couldn't take my eyes off you."

"They were designer jeans," she corrected, biting down on her lip to keep from falling under the spell of memories of her own.

"You looked so cute in that batting helmet, Jess. You'd be standing there in the batter's box, and I'd walk over and put my arms around you, pretending to show you how to hold the bat. Then I'd start kissing the back of your neck right about here." He touched the place right below his right ear.

Jessie's lips parted and her chest rose and fell beneath the thin fabric of her cotton dress. She couldn't hear the clink of the silverware that was being collected at the table next to her or the tinkling of china dishes being stacked. She wasn't in the restaurant anymore. She was back with Jarrett in New Jersey, back in his arms.

"Remember, Jess?" he asked as he reached across the forgotten steak and salad to take her hand. "Remember how we made an agreement that if we ever needed each other . . ."

Bristling, Jessie pulled away and stood. "That's history."

"A history is important to doctors." He rose and put his hand on her elbow to stop her from leaving when his attempt at humor fell flat. "Please, sit down. I'll behave."

Against her better judgement, she did.

Just then, Peggy and a few of the other nurses from the hospital came in for dinner. It had been apparent from the conversation earlier at the hospital that the life and times of Jarrett Collins was the topic of the month, so she wasn't at all surprised when Peggy stopped by their table.

"Fancy seeing you two together," she said. The glances of the nurses with her went quickly from Jessie to Jarrett. "Dr. Collins, you seem to be a fast worker—out of the emergency room as well as in it. Jessie's only been back for a day or two and already you have her cornered at Casey's." She put her hand on Jarrett's shoulder. "You should have said something after the delivery. If I had known you were hungry, I could have whipped up something for you back at my apartment."

"Jessie and I are old friends and we wanted to catch up on the last years," he quickly said.

"As long as that's all," Peggy said, visibly relaxing. "You're the first new face we've had around here in months and I'd hate to think you were already taken." Finally she took her hand from Jarrett's shoulder. "I'll see you both at the hospital." Then she moved away from their table with a farewell wave of her hand.

"It seems as though that's all I've been saying lately," Jarrett said after she left.

Jessie looked up from the lettuce leaf she had been poking with her fork. "What did you say?"

"I said it seems I've been having to explain to just about everyone in town that I knew you before."

Jessie wasn't surprised. "Do you have any idea how many times a single, or even semi-single, handsome doctor comes to a small town like Tempest?"

"You think I'm handsome?" Jarrett asked, squaring his shoulders and preening.

"Don't get over-confident," Jessie said with a laugh. "I was just commenting on the latest gossip, which, I might add, is down to a science in this town, so be careful."

"Is that right?" Jarrett could see her relaxing. "So how often does a handsome man come to Tempest?" He put a hand to his chest. "And mind you, I'm not talking about myself."

"Of course not." She was amused by his reaction. "To answer your question, hardly ever. The available women here trade information and line up for a crack at any new blood."

His low chuckle vibrated over her tingling nerve ends. "Let's see . . . who would I pick first? Maybe when I make my rounds at the hospital I can hand out numbers."

She glanced at him sharply to see if there was any mockery in his expression, but she only saw amusement deepen the edges of his mouth without turning it into a smile. Her gaze wandered downward to the white of his shirt with the top three buttons unfastened. There was a gold chain around his neck and she caught a glimpse of curly, golden chest hair. His underlying appeal was unnerving.

"Something wrong?" He'd caught her staring.

Jessie's pulse did a quick acceleration. "Yes." She sighed the admission. "Jarrett, just tell me. Why are you here in Tempest?"

"You ask me that a lot."

"If I thought you had answered the question honestly, I'd stop."

She noticed that his gaze was on the parted curve of her lips, and felt them tremble from the look that was oddly physical. Brazenly male, maddeningly confident, Jarrett had turned her quiet life on end from the moment she saw him at the hospital. He reached out and wrapped his fingers around hers, the heat of the touch jolting her. She took a slow deep breath to counter it.

"You want honesty, then honesty it is. I needed a friend after my divorce," he said quite suddenly and quite seriously. "And somehow I felt you were that friend."

"Oh." She pulled back her hand. Divorced. The obvious nearly made her crumple. "So . . ." It seemed like ages before she managed to get out the rest. "When did you get married?" She tried to appear blasé, but when she dropped her fork into her lap as she stabbed at the salad again, she knew she had failed miserably.

Jarrett pretended not to notice when Jessie slipped the fork back onto the table. "About ten years ago."

He saw surprise jolt her and added quickly. "But it wasn't what could be called a real marriage."

Jessie felt her features grow somber when she realized he must have gotten married shortly after the last time she saw him. She tucked her lower lip in between her teeth. "After all the time together, what would you call it then?" she finally asked.

"It was more like an understanding. It's hard to explain. I did try to make the best of it however."

Jessie recoiled. "Marriage isn't something to try out for a while, Jarrett. It's a serious commitment."

There was no defense for her words. "I know that. I made a mistake, Jess. A terrible mistake." Silence hung in the air between them like a shield.

It was Jessie who broke through first. "Listen, you don't have to tell me anything. It really isn't any of my business that you got married or that you came here. You can do anything you want to do. You don't need my permission."

"My divorce isn't a secret, and coming to Tempest was something I had to do. I wanted to see you again."

Jessie felt a frown of confusion crease her forehead. "How did you know I'd still be here?"

"I didn't."

"Then weren't you taking a big chance of signing on to the staff of a small town hospital for nothing?"

"It wouldn't have been for nothing. I love practicing medicine no matter where I do it. I felt I needed a change from the pace of the big city, and I remembered how much you loved living in the Midwest. I thought it was as good a place as any to start over." His voice finally sparkled again. "Finding out that you were still around was an added perk."

"You certainly presume a lot, Dr. Collins." She

turned her face away from him so he couldn't read the turmoil in her eyes.

"Such as?"

She swung her head back to face him. "Such as thinking that you can just walk back into my life again and pick up where you left off when you walked out."

"I never assumed I could pick up where I left off, but you did say you were glad to see me." His voice hinted at skepticism. "Did you mean it?"

Her mouth opened and closed twice while she thought of a safe answer. "You took me by surprise. What did you expect me to say?"

"Honestly, I wasn't sure what you'd do."

Jessie colored slightly. There was almost a panic inside her that made her feel shaky. "I used to get so angry at you for leaving me so abruptly. There were times that I wanted to drive out East, smack you in the head, and ask you what in the world you were thinking. You left me open to questions and talk. My friends and family remembered how we always said we were going to get marr . . ." Realizing where the words were leading, she stopped suddenly and dropped her eyes to her hands.

But Jarrett knew what she would have said. He studied the way her ponytail fell softly around her shoulders when she lowered her head and his heart thundered heavily. He wondered if his own disappointment showed as openly as hers. It should. He'd been thoroughly discouraged with life, love, and marriage in New York. He balled his hands into fists and held them stiffly at his sides. If he didn't, he knew he would take her in his arms and hold her.

"I wish I could make it all up to you. You deserved more," he finally said.

Jessie's throat constricted a little. "I've been happy."

"I hope so." For a long moment, neither of them moved. "Well," Jarrett said, dropping his hands on the table, the noise making Jessie jump, "that was a lot harder than I thought it was going to be."

Jessie furrowed her brow. "What was?"

"Clearing the first hurdle in getting to know each other again."

It was on the tip of her tongue to say that it was really too soon to tell, but the hope in his eyes made her resist the impulse. "Well maybe we did," she conceded, simply, and picked at the half-eaten steak on her plate while absently glancing at the gold watch looped around her wrist. Her eyes widened when she saw the time. "It's getting late. I have a ton of paperwork to do." She laid the fork down and reached for the check the waitress had left, but Jarrett was faster. Her fingers ended up tangling briefly with his, the contact sending a tingle up her arm.

"I asked you to dinner, remember?" he reminded her, reaching for his wallet.

"At least let me get the tip."

"No, it's my treat," he said, walking with her to the cashier. He dug out his wallet from a back pocket in his jeans and paid the cheek. "And I didn't mean to antagonize you tonight, Jess."

"I guess I know that," Jessie said softly. Each step they took as they walked into the parking lot only made her more aware of him. "But don't take things for granted, either," she said.

"Are you afraid that's why I'm here?" He took a step closer to her.

Yes was not a smart answer, so she didn't say it. "What do you want from me, Jarrett?"

He sighed, but never hesitated. "This."

His arms suddenly scooped around her and pulled her to him. She made a protesting sound as his mouth met hers in a slow, tentative kiss. His hand reached up and cupped her jaw, the kiss deepening when she did not pull away.

She grabbed the front of his shirt, her hands twisting around the material, and she hung on for dear life. Suspended now between disbelief and enchantment, her heart took a perilous leap and she kissed him back, telling herself that everything was happening so fast and she didn't have time to be rational. Being in his arms was having a disastrous effect on her resistance. The scrape of the evening shadow of his beard against her cheek sent a delightful arc of prickles through her. She felt the inherent strength of his kiss, yet also the incredible gentleness with which he molded his lips to hers. She breathed in his masculine scent and threaded her fingers through his hair.

"Hmmm," she said from somewhere deep in her throat.

"Hmmm," he responded, hugging her tightly. He pulled his mouth away from hers just enough to talk. "I think we're about to catch up on a few more memories if we aren't careful."

Embarrassed, Jessie pushed herself away. She hadn't expected such a strong reaction after all these years, and suspected that neither had he. She stepped back tensely. "I think I've walked down memory lane far enough for one night." She let her glance move to his eyes and saw longing. "And apparently, so have you."

Jarrett walked slowly up the brick walk to his condo. He put the key in the lock and opened the front door, wondering if he would ever get used to the feeling of coming home to an empty house. In the living room he flipped on the lights and turned on the TV. After tossing his coat over the chair, he eased himself onto the sofa and stretched his arms across the back.

Although he hadn't been sure if Jessie would still be in town, he did come to Tempest specifically to find her. He'd fantasized about seeing her again, and even dreamed that she would be divorced and unhappy like him, so he could rush to her rescue and they could both forget what he'd done to her.

But it seemed he was not going to ride in on a white charger and become her Prince Charming; he was too blackened for that. And she was not going to welcome him with open arms. She was angry. But that wasn't all bad. Anger was better than ambivalence.

Ten years ago they were so close that he knew everything about her. He came to Tempest armed with that knowledge. But just this evening he realized he was missing even the basics, and there was a lot more that he didn't know from the years he had let slip by him.

Did she ever get married? Did she still like chocolate better than anything else in the world? Did she still sleep with kneesocks on in the summer? Did champagne still make her hiccup? Did she still have that little tickle spot on her waist?

A hot ache grew inside him. Maybe he should have thought this whole thing through a little more. True, they had made some wonderful memories, and he'd thought about them often enough, especially lately. But he upset her today by bringing up the past when she clearly wanted to forget it.

He told her the truth about what had happened while they were apart. True, maybe he diluted it a bit, but he didn't know how to tell her how he had failed them both. He barely believed it himself. How could he expect her to?

He closed his eyes and laid his head back on the padded sofa back. Tomorrow. Tomorrow he'd try to explain it to her.

But for now, he would think about Jessie. Jessie O'Brien, that skinny girl in tight designer jeans who could hit a baseball a mile and wanted to be a ballerina. And Jessie O'Brien the beautiful, intelligent woman who he felt tremble and surrender in his arms when he kissed her only a few moments earlier.

Jessie lay curled in her bed under a thick quilt with blue argyle socks on her feet and the air conditioner running full blast. It was going to be a long night. She knew she wouldn't be able to sleep. The memories were simply too clear now.

Why couldn't she have reacted like some other women who saw their former boyfriends? Those women could chat with old flames, calmly discussing their work and interests and other, new loves.

But Jessie hadn't really had other loves, new or otherwise. She'd dated, half-heartedly, but it was hard to admit that after all these years the best she had done since Jarrett was a six-month fling with a guy who eventually left her to find himself in a California commune.

She was in her thirties now. Wasn't this supposed to be the most sensual time of her life? Wasn't she supposed to be enjoying wild nights of even wilder passion married to the man of her dreams while their children slept in rooms down the hall in their two-story custom-built home?

She pulled the pillow out from under her head and

molded it around her face. He was the man of her dreams. No more questions, no more wondering. Now he was back, and maybe she had a second chance.

But the question was, did she have the courage to take it?

Chapter Three

If there was one thing Jessie didn't need, it was to be distracted by Jarrett at work on the day she set aside to reconcile a huge stack of past-due bills. His voice sailed through the air as he spoke to someone in the hallway outside her office door telling her that he was close, very close.

The sound of his rich laugh made her stomach tighten with the anticipation. For some reason she didn't want him to see the mess on her desk so she scooped up the bills and dropped them into the top right-hand drawer. Before closing it, she sighed. The large number of bills she had to catch up on was largely her fault. No account went into collection if she could help it. She spent a good part of each day poring over details and arranging payment schedules that could be kept by families.

People who could not pay their bills were not merely account numbers to her. She saw it as no less than a small miracle when someone recovered from an illness, and she wasn't about to let the joy of that miracle be overshadowed by the worry of paying the huge bills that often accompanied the cure.

Jarrett's throaty laugh lifted her attention back to the doorway. In another second he stepped inside her office. Her pulse started fluttering crazily as he approached her desk. Tall and lean, flashing that great smile; she felt weaker with each step he took. The whiteness of his lab coat contrasted sharply with his deeply tanned skin and the black stethoscope he had draped around his neck, but her senses had no respect for the profession he had chosen. They were all reacting to his raw masculinity, his handsome features, and his incredible eyes.

"Hello, Jarrett." Jessie was amazed that her voice hadn't cracked like a giddy schoolgirl when she spoke.

His eyes crinkled at the corners when he smiled at her. "Have you been hiding from me?"

"No." She dipped her head to one side, her blond hair swinging free. "I've just been busy with work and with the fund-raising for the squad."

"How's it going?" Placing both hands on her desk, he lounged casually against it.

"I'm up to my eyebrows in past-due accounts and we're only about halfway to our goal with only a few weeks left in the drive."

"Sounds like all work and no play."

"For a while," Jessie admitted. "But I'm treating myself to a little R-and-R this evening."

"Oh? Have a date?"

Jessie frowned for a minute while she contemplated her answer. In a town like Tempest, if she said she had a date, she had better be ready to produce one.

"No." She hoped her voice sounded like it didn't matter.

Jarrett straightened and slapped his hands together. "Well you do now. I rented a video. We can watch it together."

She almost jumped at the invitation but managed to appear casual. "I was really planning to make it an early night."

"No problem." He dropped into a chair facing her. "I'll bring take-out and then after the movie, I'm gone." He crossed his heart with his index finger and held his right hand in the air. "Promise."

Jessie gave him a short, level look. "I'd love to take you up on that, but you know, in a small town like this, and with us having a history, it won't be long before rumor would have it all over town that we're dating."

"Really?" She saw amusement come into his eyes as he leaned forward in the chair. "That could be arranged," he volunteered.

She wished he wasn't so close. The tangy scent of his after-shave surrounded her. "Can the new doctor in town afford to have that kind of talk going around?"

"I've been the object of empty talk before." He shrugged his shoulders indifferently. "It doesn't bother me."

"You haven't been the talk of Tempest, yet."

He held up his hands. "Can't be any different than back home. So, what do you say? Take-out? A movie?"

Jessie had run out of arguments. "I suppose a movie would be relaxing. As long as it's not one of those shoot-em-up, gory, alien-police-army adventures."

"Agreed. Now what would you like to eat? Pizza? Chinese?"

"Pizza would be fine."

"Be there at six?"

"Better make it seven. I have a desk full of . . ." The roar of her name interrupted the sentence.

"Jessie, what on earth were you thinking when you agreed to these terms?" Gordon Burrows, her boss, exploded into the room. He was a big man with silver hair, dark blue eyes, and a frown Jessie always thought was there to hide the fact that he wasn't really as gruff as he appeared to be. "At ten dollars a month, it's going to take Hartford fifteen years to pay off his seventeen-hundred-dollar balance!" He shoved the installment papers toward her.

Jessie didn't back down. "Actually, fourteen years and two months." She resisted the urge to give him the 'but-at-least-the-hospital-is-getting-paid' explanation. "I know it's not the norm, but we're saving him from . . ."

Gordon made a face. "Miss O'Brien, I can't save *everyone*."

Jessie's mouth tightened as she looked up into his set features and fixed eyes. "You didn't. The surgical team did, and I'm just trying to make sure he doesn't have to worry so much about paying for it that he ends back here with cardiac arrest and an even bigger bill."

Burrows was opening his mouth to say something else when Jarrett stood and stepped around the desk, extending his hand as he spoke. "Gordon Burrows, isn't it? I've been meaning to see you."

Burrows finally noticed someone else was in the room. He narrowed his eyes and took Jarrett's hand. "And you are?"

"Jarrett Collins."

Burrows nodded. "Ah yes, Mike Lombardi called me just this morning and asked if I'd met you yet."

Jarrett turned back to Jessie. "Mike Lombardi is the Chief Financial Officer at New York General, and a close friend of mine. He knew I was looking for a new focus. Apparently in passing, Mr. Burrows told him about the opening here."

"In passing nothing," Gordon said in his usual disconnected voice. "A few months ago at the convention in St. Louis, he locked me into a sixteen-hour poker game. Not only did I miss the seminar on the new rules concerning Medicaid payments, but he nearly cleaned out my wallet too."

"A break for me," Jarrett said. "Otherwise I might have ended up in some nice, quiet town in Iowa instead."

"Play poker, Collins?" Burrows asked.

"A little."

"Lombardi ever get you back in New York?"

Jarrett held up his hands in a defensive posture. "Just once. After that, I was only a silent observer."

Burrows stepped into the hallway. "Stop by sometime, Collins. I could tell you stories that would curl your hair."

When he was gone, Jessie grimaced. "Thanks for the rescue. I thought I was in for another battle."

"Seems like a worthy cause."

"It is. The patient owing the past-due bill Gordon was screaming about was in for a triple bypass six months ago."

"Costly operation, but well worth the price. And it's not such a big balance due. Why did Burrows get so upset?"

"Mr. Hartford was laid off from his job over a year ago and can't seem to find work." Jessie tossed her head. "This area isn't exactly a booming metropolis. Anyway, his medical bills cleaned out the family savings account and still didn't cover everything. The family didn't want the bill to go to collection."

"And Burrows doesn't understand that."

"I think he does. Actually, I even think he likes the idea that I set up the payment schedules and he gets to grumble about them." She smiled. "It lets him off the hook."

Jarrett laughed, and immediately Jessie wished he hadn't. She could never resist his laugh. It was warm, full-bodied, and genuine and it made her remember how easy it would be for the old attraction to pull her back to him.

He gave her a knowing smile. "You always were a softy when it came to disasters."

She colored slightly. "I was not."

"Really?" He appeared to work hard to pretend to be stunned. "I remember quite vividly when your Aunt Judy sent me a newspaper clipping of you chained to a tree . . ."

She cut him off. "The tree was two hundred years old and the town was just going to chop it down in order to widen the road."

"What about the time you took up the fight to get recycling containers in the park?" He threw back his head and let out a great peal of laughter. "I teased you for months about being a member of the garbage police. And there was . . ."

She held up a hand. "Okay, but this is different."

He grinned. "Some philosophy." His voice was smooth, his gaze steady. "You care."

Jessie sat back in her chair. "There are more important things than money." She studied his unwavering eyes. "And I think you agree. If you didn't, you wouldn't be here in Tempest. You would still be in New York."

"You're right," he said reluctantly. He glanced at his watch. "I better not hang around here and keep you from your work any longer. I'll see you tonight." He turned his smile up a notch. "Seven, right?"

"Right."

As Jarrett left Jessie felt her heartbeat begin to fall to a more normal rate. She shook her head. Her reaction to him was reason enough to underscore the fact that she should not jump into things too quickly and assume Jarrett wanted something permanent this time.

It was also reason enough for her to want to do just that.

Precisely at seven, Jessie's doorbell sounded. Jarrett stood there balancing a pizza in one hand and a videocassette in the other. He'd changed from a shirt and tie into jeans and a T-shirt. And he was smiling.

"Hi." He handed her the pizza box and took a long, lazy scan of her from head to toe. "Hungry?"

"A little." Jessie's fingers dug into the box. The telltale collapse of cardboard was the only thing that made her relax them. "Come in." She turned and began walking to the kitchen. From behind her she heard the door click closed and her heart jerked with it. "Want something to drink?" she asked, purely to center herself again.

Jarrett dropped onto the couch and slid the video onto the coffee table. Leaning back, he slipped his arm across the sofa back. "Whatever you're having is fine." He leaned forward and peered at the VCR. "How does this video thing work? Some of them are more complicated than brain surgery."

Jessie handed him two glasses of iced tea. "I'll do it." She reached for the tape. "What did you rent?"

He put the glasses on the coffee table and rose to

stand beside her, resisting the urge to touch her hair, knowing it would be a mistake. He handed her the video. "*Major League.* Have you seen it?"

"It's one of my favorites." As she slid the tape into the machine and turned on the TV, Jarrett returned to the couch.

"It reminds me a little of us," he said, sitting back down.

She hesitated only briefly. "How so?"

"Baseball, a girl, a guy who messed up the romance." He moved the table and stretched the toes of his sneakers toward the TV. "Don't you agree?"

She ignored his smirk. "Maybe a little," she said, pressing the play button.

"At the end, the guy gets the girl back," Jarrett reminded her.

"Movies are supposed to have a happy ending."

"That's exactly what I had in mind, too," he said, picking up one of the glasses. "A toast then. To happily-ever-after."

Jessie picked up her glass and raised it to her lips. "In the movie, you mean," she said.

He raised his glass higher. "For starters."

Moving to the sofa, she sat down. As the movie began, she found she could not tear her eyes away from him. She felt the tension grow inside her. She knew she couldn't put off any longer what had to be said.

"It was a little weird to come back from vacation and find you here in Tempest," she said.

There was a long pause as Jarrett slid closer to her. He set his glass on the table. "To tell you the truth, until the last minute, I never expected to go through with moving here."

He studied her again until Jessie felt like begging

him to stop. She struggled to keep her features composed. "Maybe this isn't such a good idea."

"I didn't come here to upset you. My life is in such a mess. I just felt I couldn't get it straightened out until I talked to you."

Jessie put down her glass and sighed. She dropped her chin and turned back to him slowly, very slowly, before raising her gaze and allowing him to look at her. "Jarrett, if you came here to find the girl you left behind, I'm sorry to have to disappoint you, but she's gone," she said, the movie continuing in front of them, unwatched and unheard.

Jarrett shook his head. "No, I don't think I came here looking for her. I think I came here looking for me."

She looked at him. He appeared tired beyond his years. She suddenly didn't think she wanted to know. "I have no right to dig into your past."

"Yes you do. More than you even realize." He snatched his glass, downing the rest of the tea in one swallow.

"Jarrett, it's been ten years. We've both moved on."

"But you want to know. I can see it in your eyes. You want to hear why I walked out on you as badly as I need to tell you." He leaned toward her so she would not miss a word. "I left you because of me." He waited for her to react. When she didn't he went on. "I guess that sounds rather absurd, but it's the truth, Jessie."

After a full minute of silence she asked very quietly, "Exactly what do you mean by that?"

He sucked in a huge gulp of air and let it out. "I left you because I was selfish." He closed his eyes. "I was going off to medical school. Long years of internship and residency were looming. I wanted to be

a doctor so badly that I didn't want any distractions."
He dropped his head, opened his eyes, and stared at
her hand resting on her knee.

"I was a distraction?" she asked in a whisper. For
years she imagined his explanation and how she would
feel when he told her. Now the emotions his words
unleashed were exploding with such force that she was
nowhere near prepared to handle them.

Jarrett's hand encircled hers loosely. His thumb
rubbed across her knuckles. "Yes. I loved you, but
with all the hard work ahead, all the time I would have
to devote to medicine, I didn't think I could learn to
be a good doctor and give you the life you deserved
too."

"Why didn't you let me help decide that?" she
asked in a small voice.

His sad smile was still aimed at her hand. "I've
asked myself that question a thousand times over the
years." His gaze moved up to her face. "And I never
got the same answer twice."

"But you got married, Jarrett. And apparently not
too long after you were in medical school." Her voice
trailed away and she pulled her hand from his. It was
hard for her to admit that while she waited, and hoped,
and dreamed, he was busy with a career and a wife.
"It was as though I never mattered."

Pulling her hand from his, she got to her feet. He
leapt up after her. "You did matter. You mattered very
much."

"If I did, you wouldn't have run off and married
someone else!" She turned away and wrapped her
arms around her mid-section for warmth.

"Jess, you'll never know how sorry I am that that
happened."

"Don't try to apologize. That's not going to make everything okay."

Gently he put his hand on her shoulder, but dropped it to his side when she flinched at the contact. "Please, turn around and look at me."

Jessie's voice was barely discernible as she murmured, "It doesn't make sense, Jarrett. You said you loved me, yet a few months after you went off to school you got married. Why?"

He touched her again. This time she turned slowly to him. "Do you want the truth or a polite lie?"

She looked deeply into his eyes. "I might not want the truth, but I need it."

He stiffened. "I married her because she was the daughter of the director of the school." He swallowed. His lips opened but no sound came out. After several seconds, in a strangled voice, he said the words he knew might cleave them apart for good. "And because she convinced me that we were in love."

She dropped back to the sofa as though someone had hit her full force in the stomach. Growing up, he seemed to carefully couch his decisions with facts, even to the point of apparently thinking through their relationship very carefully. He never seemed like someone who would jump blindly into anything, especially something as serious as marriage. Could she have been wrong about him all those years before? As they were growing, was she the only one who thought they would end up together someday?

"That's not a reason to marry anyone," she managed to say.

He dropped down next to her, their eyes meeting as he spoke. "It's a very long story."

She bowed her head to hide the pain she knew showed in her eyes. The building tears burned, but she refused to allow them to fall. "You must have loved her." She didn't want to know, but found she couldn't control the words.

"At times I thought I did." He ran a hand through his hair, watching her face as she tried to compose it. "Heck, I don't know for sure."

"How could you marry her if you didn't love her?"

"There are a lot of reasons why people do what they do; some right and some wrong," he admitted with regret.

Nervously Jessie stood and walked away. Jarrett followed her. "Do you still think of her?" she asked quietly, knowing she could not just erase ten years of commitment to another person from her life or memory very easily. The gnawing fear that he would leave again began to grow.

Jarrett's face closed. He sighed heavily and shook his head. "It's hard not to." He drew his hand down his face, covering his mouth for a minute before answering. The marriage had been a terrible mistake, he knew that. But how could he tell Jessie about what had happened when he wasn't even sure himself?

Jessie tore her gaze from the turmoil mirrored in his eyes and looked at his cheerless mouth. "I understand. She was part of your life for a long time."

He nodded. "The memories aren't always pleasant, but I'm learning to live with them," he said shakily.

She looked at him and felt he was holding something back. Reaching out, she pressed her palm to his cheek. When she touched him, for a moment, she felt as though she was sharing his pain and it hurt for her to breathe. "You don't have say any more. Not tonight." She couldn't understand why there was so much pain in her own chest. There was nothing between them anymore. Or was there? The cocky confidence he walked in with seemed to have left him, replaced by pain that was reflected in his features. She wanted to help, but didn't know how.

He took her hand from his cheek and held it to his chest. "Jess, I feel so guilty."

"About what?"

"All of it. It seems every decision I made hurt someone." He let go of her hand and blew out a long breath to steady himself. "This is more than what I had had in mind for a first date. Maybe I'd better go."

Jessie turned away so he would not see the turmoil in her eyes. She pressed her lips together, unsure of what to do or say next to save them both.

Neither moved. Jarrett studied the back of her hair and the wrinkles on her green blouse where it had pressed against the couch. "Do you think there's some way we can work this out?" he managed to say.

She balled her hands into fists until the nails dug into the soft skin of her palm. "I don't know what to say, Jarrett. It's a lot for me to handle."

"I didn't come here to hurt you, Jess." He turned her by the elbow and said nothing more as she studied the top button on his shirt instead of looking him in the eye.

"I know," she said softly.

"I wish none of it had happened. But it did. I don't think either of us can ignore that."

He leaned closer to her and Jessie saw that he wanted to kiss her. She pressed a hand to his chest and felt his heart drum crazily. Her heart was doing the same. Suddenly she wanted his kiss, wanted it more than she wanted to breathe. Rising on tiptoe, she brushed her lips lightly across his.

When she broke the kiss, Jarrett moved back and stood perfectly still. She looked at his mouth and watched his lips curve into a sad smile. Before her brain could engage the rational part of her that would normally say go slowly, her heart took over. Her arms encircled his neck and their eyes met, smoky green and china blue, questioning, remembering.

"Jessie," he murmured. "I've missed you more than you could know."

Old familiar feelings began to emerge from deep within Jessie's heart, and the urge to keep kissing him became almost unbearable. "Jarrett, we shouldn't be doing this. It's too soon."

"Maybe," he brushed his lips across hers once, twice, "we never should have stopped."

Jessie could barely think. Jarrett had taught her how to kiss when they were both teenagers. Then his kisses were those of first love: timid and awkward. Now he was a man, and his kisses had improved.

"I need you, Jess," he whispered, almost desperately. "I've always needed you. I guess I've only begun to realize just how much."

His kisses drew memories from her she thought she had forgotten. She thought about what it would be like for them again. And the thought scared her half to death.

Heart still pounding erratically in her chest, she broke away. She lifted her chin and nearly drowned in the hooded green of his eyes. "Jarrett," she said firmly, but in a voice that was merely a whisper.

"Jess," his voice overlapped hers, "what are we going to do about this thing between us? We can't go on sparring forever."

Jessie shook her head in response. It felt good, knowing he still wanted to be with her after all these years, but it hurt not knowing why he really did. Was she just someone from a time in his past that was kinder, safer—a time without responsibilities—or did he mean what he said? She had to be careful, very careful. Once she had believed that they belonged together, but she wasn't going to pin her future to a dream again. This time it had to be real. She had to be sure.

"We were only supposed to watch a movie and eat pizza," she said in response to his question.

His eyes darkened and his smile faded. "You're right. I was stupid." He ran a finger down her nose and across her lips. "I did promise to behave. But it isn't finished between us," he cautioned. "I think you know that." He kissed her lightly on the cheek. "Good night, Jess." He paused at the door and then left without a backward glance.

How long she stayed in the living room lost in memories she didn't know. When the clock struck midnight, she realized she had to get some sleep.

Once in bed, she tossed and turned. Her hands shook as she turned on the light. There had been a surprising moment when she had really looked at him, had seen his vulnerable side, and it had nearly been her undoing. But she couldn't let that weaken her resolve. She sensed he knew how much it had hurt her when he left her so many years earlier. He couldn't possibly expect her to welcome him back with open arms.

She lay back down and stared at the ceiling, thinking about all that had happened in such a short amount of time. Just before she drifted off to sleep, she found herself thinking about how easy it would be to trust him again.

And how easy it would be for him to hurt her if she did.

Chapter Four

The ambulance lurched sharply to the left and skidded around a slow-moving car, sending the sunglasses set on the dashboard tumbling to the floor. Jessie yanked the steering wheel hard to the right in a sudden compensating movement that lifted the hair lying thickly against her neck, creating a fleeting cooling effect in the August heat of the cab.

"Not only is the air conditioner still broken, but I suppose the ambulance is now invisible," she muttered. She pressed a button, producing a shrill blast from the siren. She smiled when the whistle sent the remaining cars scurrying to the shoulder of the road. But the hot midwestern day didn't make her feel the heat. The race to the hospital from the devastation caused by a three-car accident on Route 87 out by the shopping plaza turned up the temperature for her.

"Jessie," Matt called out from the back. "How much

longer? This little girl needs more help than I can give her here."

"About ten minutes. How's she doing?" Jessie called back.

"Stable for now, but she's lost a lot of blood. The heat in here is making it difficult for her to breathe even with my help. When's the air conditioner getting fixed?"

"Who knows. What we need to do is raise enough money for a new rig," Jessie shot back, slowing the vehicle as she approached another intersection. She set off another shrill siren blast and checked in both directions before speeding across.

"Good thing we were at the shopping center collecting for the fund drive when the call about the accident came in," Matt said, placing the stethoscope in his ears and pumping up the small vinyl cuff that was wrapped around the child's thin arm. He looked down at her pale face and shook his head. "This girl was bounced around pretty badly before she was thrown out of the car. I'll bet she didn't have her seat belt on."

"Just keep her alive, Matt," Jessie replied, a hint of pleading in her voice. No one ever died in her ambulance, and if she had her way, no one ever would. "We're almost there." She bit down on her lip, trying to remember if the construction on Eighteenth Street was scheduled to begin this week or next. She didn't need a road delay for a detour. Time was precious when dealing with the first few minutes of trauma.

A lot of people, some of her co-workers and fellow squad members included, didn't understand why she was so obsessed with the fact that no one had ever died in her ambulance en route to the hospital. When asked why it was so important to her, Jessie's response was a declaration of duty and a love for people. But that was only partly true. No one suspected the real root of her dedication. She hadn't even come to realize it herself until a few years ago.

When her fantasy of a family and a happily ever after with the man of her dreams faded, it left her cold inside. She looked for a reason to feel warm again, and found it by volunteering at the local rescue squad. Now she used her spare time to make sure that those involved in their own tussle with misfortune got the extra few minutes they needed to allow them to be able to make their own wishes and dreams come true.

But now Jarrett had come back into her life. And the emptiness she had learned to control after he left threatened to grow into something big and real and defiant. She pushed it once again out of her mind.

"Talk to me, Matt," she called out after a long silence began to make her feel edgy. "How's she doing?"

"She's hanging in there, Jess. Just get us there."

"A few more minutes," she replied, responding to the urgency in his voice. "How are her vitals?"

"Stable for now. She's got a chance."

Matt and another paramedic continued to monitor the girl's vital signs as the ambulance, siren screaming, reached the entrance to the trauma unit. Jessie slid the vehicle into the reserved space in front and turned off the engine. Almost immediately, the hospital doors flew open and a cascade of white uniformed people, including Jarrett, descended on the van.

"What happened?" he asked, running toward them.

"Bad accident near the Interstate," Matt responded, jumping from the back of the ambulance to help remove the stretcher.

"How many injuries?" Instinctively Jarrett got into

step opposite Matt. Only then did he see that the patient was a child. Her head was wrapped in a soft crown of white bandages already stained a bright red in one spot. For a fraction of a heartbeat, he felt numb. His feet moved as though they were encased in hardening cement, and he forgot to breathe. His hand trembled as he reached down toward her. At the contact, he went on full automatic, and his training took over.

"Run it down for me, Matt," he ordered, pulling on some latex gloves as the gurney was wheeled into an examining room.

"BP 90 over 60, pulse 160, airway clear, but she's unconscious. I'm pretty sure this little one wasn't wearing her seat belt," Matt replied, shifting to help lift the small girl onto a stretcher in the room.

"On three," Jarrett said, nodding to the other members of the trauma team and placing his hands under the child's body. As a fluid unit, they transferred her to the hospital stretcher.

When he cut away the temporary bandage, Jarrett could see deep, irregular gashes running across the girl's forehead. Pieces of bone and tissue showed through jagged edges of skin. "She must have hit the windshield pretty hard. Get me the works," he said to the nurse drawing blood. "Someone get the portable X ray unit in here."

Mentally processing the information as it was updated for him, Jarrett formulated a plan of action he felt comfortable with even before the entire dressing was removed. "Good thing you got her here quickly, Matt," he acknowledged as he continued to work on the child. "It just might have saved her life."

"That's Jess for you," Matt said as he prepared to leave. "She always makes sure they get here in time."

"Jessie's here?" Jarrett glanced briefly toward the

window, but continued treatment without breaking rhythm.

"Outside wrapping up the paperwork."

"Ask her to wait, will you?" Matt nodded as he left.

Jarrett looked down at the little girl. "Where are her parents?" he asked. "More suction."

A nurse handed him a sponge. "Her mother was driving. The impact wedged her in the car. They're still trying to contact her father."

Jarrett gently dabbed at the injury with a sponge. "Any word on the mother's injuries? Sponge."

"First reports say she's a little battered and bruised, but she'll be okay." Peggy moved into place next to Jarrett and dabbed at the child's skin while another nurse slapped the next instrument Jarrett requested into his outstretched hand. "She should be here any minute now."

"Bet she had her seat belt on," Jarrett said, shaking his head. "This little one's mother should have made sure both belts were fastened before she moved the car." This is her fault, he thought as he worked. Then almost as quickly, he pushed the reflection from his head. No, he wouldn't allow himself to think that. It was no one's fault. It was an accident. There was no sense adding to the guilt the mother was undoubtedly feeling right now. A sudden chill ran through him with the thought, nearly making his hand shake again while he gently probed the wound. Guilt. He certainly knew that feeling.

"Check her reflexes again," he said, briefly lifting his attention from the head wound to catch a nurse's eye with the request. "I want to keep an eye on her motor functions. And someone get on that lacerated arm." He stepped back just long enough for the portable X ray unit to take a shot of her head.

Guilt. The word rolled back into his mind during the brief pause. His life seemed to be haunted by guilt lately; for the house he built without Jesse and for marrying a woman he really didn't love. Sometimes the choices he had made in his life made him question his medical skills. Could he count on his ability to make the right choices now?

He looked down at the small girl beneath him and shrugged out his dark thoughts. He was not going to let this little one die.

"Has anyone found her father yet?" he asked. When no one answered, he continued. "Someone find out for me, please. This little girl is going to be scared when she regains consciousness. I'd like both parents there when she wakes up." Peggy hurried to comply with the request.

It was at times like this, when he was treating children who had been brought to him after an accident that made Jarrett feel the most susceptible to attacks of conscience and honorability. He might be a good doctor. He might even be an enlightened, intelligent man. But he had been a pretty lousy husband. As a mater of fact, it was the only point on which he and his ex-wife agreed when she slapped him with the divorce papers.

The long, drawn-out court fight drained him physically, emotionally, and financially, making him feel a failure as a man. He shook his head, sending the demons temporarily scattering back to the past where they belonged. This was neither the time nor the place for thoughts like that.

Fortunately, at that moment, one of the nurses burst back into the room and held the X ray of the child's head in front of the overhead light. Jarrett squinted into the brightness and studied the film as he stripped off his latex gloves.

"Who's the neurosurgeon on call?" He asked, as the flurry of activity around the child continued.

"Silberberg, I think," someone answered him.

"Call him. It looks like a little piece of her skull has been imbedded in the brain. We have to get it out to keep the cortex from swelling."

"Is she going to make it?" one of the nurses asked.

"I hope so, but I'll know for sure once we operate. Take her upstairs and get her prepped. Stat." He took two steps toward the door and stopped. "And tell Dr. Silberberg that I want to assist on this one."

Jessie filled a paper cup with hot coffee and scalded her dry throat with it as she drank. Her stomach was rolling. She pressed a steadying hand to it. Accidents involving children were the worst ones for her. She had learned to handle adults—put the extent of their injuries out of her mind—but it was the children who affected her the most.

There were other people in the waiting room. One woman waited patiently with her nose pressed into a paperback. Another riffled through some magazines on the table. Jessie nodded to them. She began to pace, and wondered how anyone could stay in a room like this and not go slowly crazy. She moved around the room and prayed for the little girl.

"Jessie."

She turned toward the voice. "Jarrett, is she going to be all right?"

"She's holding her own, but we need to operate. Dr. Silberberg is up there already, and I'm on my way."

With a nod, Jessie went back to her pacing. Jarrett fell into step beside her. "I feel so useless," Jessie said.

Jarrett stopped her and slipped an arm around her shoulders. "Don't. Getting her here quickly probably saved her life." He led her to a chair and made her sit. "I understand that's a priority of yours."

Distress raced through her, but Jarrett's arms around her muted some of it. His touch was one of comfort, and she could feel his warmth, his strength. His grip tightened imperceptibly. She opened her mouth to speak just as a woman with a bandage across her forehead and a sling cradling her left arm burst into the room.

"Sandy. Where's Sandy?" Tears flowed down the woman's face. She turned to Jarrett. "Are you the doctor? Please. I need to see her." When Jarrett turned toward her, small bloodstains on his scrubs made the color drain from her face. "Oh, no."

Jarrett caught the woman as her knees buckled. Jessie quickly took her hand. "Please sit down. If you pass out, you'll be of no help to your daughter."

"I only looked away for a minute. Sandy wanted me to see the picture she was coloring." She burst into tears.

Jarrett cradled her against his shoulder for a moment. He then guided to her a chair and allowed her sobs to subside before speaking. "I'm Dr. Collins. I worked on your daughter when they brought her in."

The child's mother twisted a tattered tissue between the fingers of her right hand. "I want to see her."

"Not yet. She needs surgery."

"No!" she screamed, jumping to her feet and heading for the hallway. "I have to be with her."

Jarrett easily beat her to the doorway and stopped with a hand to her shoulder. "You can't see her. Not yet."

Jessie quickly joined them. "I'm Jessie O'Brien, the

ambulance driver. I brought your daughter in. You're Mrs. Wilson, right?"

The child's mother turned to Jessie and nodded. "I have to tell her I'm sorry. I only looked away for a minute. I have to tell her that." Tears flowed down her face as she spoke.

"You can tell her when she wakes up," Jarrett said cautiously. "Dr. Silberberg is operating, and he's the best."

"When can I see her?" The child's mother wiped her eyes with the back of her free hand.

"You can wait in the surgical waiting room on the fourth floor and I'll come for you when she's in recovery. I'll know more then. We'll do everything we can for her."

"Promise me that you will?" She reached out and grabbed onto Jarrett's arm. "And promise me you won't let her die." Her fingers tightened like a vise.

Jarrett bit down on his lip. He couldn't do that. He'd made promises like that before. Promises he couldn't keep.

Jessie sensed something was wrong. "Mrs. Wilson, I'll take you upstairs to the waiting room and stay with you until your husband arrives." She reached out to remove the fingers from around Jarrett's arm and was surprised to find that he was shaking. Her eyes met his and she could swear she saw a flash of grief. "Is there anyone else you want me to call?" she asked, returning her attention to the girl's mother.

"Yes. Her grandmother. She lives in St. Paul."

"Can you give me the number?"

"Yes." But she only stood there, crying.

Moving with her to the couch, Jessie spoke in low tones. Nodding, the woman answered. Jessie tore a piece of paper from the inside of a magazine and waited while the woman scribbled the number on it. After a moment, she patted Mrs. Wilson's shoulder in reassurance as an orderly took her upstairs.

"She feels responsible," Jessie said softly, moving with Jarrett into the hallway. "She thinks that if she were paying more attention to the road . . ."

"She should have been," Jarrett said abruptly. "And she should have made sure the girl's seat belt was buckled before she even started the engine. Parents need to be more responsible for their children."

Jessie was taken aback by his words. "What's wrong? You were wonderful with her in there and now you sound like judge and jury." The words were hardly out of her mouth when she saw a doctor in surgical scrubs approaching.

"Dr. Collins, we're ready in OR three."

Jessie saw Jarrett's face tense. "I have to go," he said.

Jessie looked toward the waiting room. "I better make that call." She turned and walked back inside.

Jarrett let her go. As much as she needed to know, he couldn't explain it all to her now anyway. Besides, there was a little girl upstairs who needed him more.

Jessie dialed the number the child's mother gave her and waited for someone to answer, feeling enormously confused at the array of emotions Jarrett had just displayed. There was something that bothered her about what he said. Doctors rarely displayed emotion like that during an emergency and never until after the patient was stabilized and off the floor.

She had no time to think about what it was, however. A gentle older voice came on the other end of the telephone.

*   *   *

It was nearly eight when Jessie got back to her apartment. Rubbing the back of her neck to loosen the tight muscles, she stepped out of her shoes and tossed her purse onto the table. If she planned on keeping her volunteer job in the rescue squad, she was going to have to get used to running into Jarrett on a regular basis; there was no way to avoid it. Life had sure gotten pretty complicated in a very short time.

She'd back out of the volunteer work if she could. One thing she had learned over the years was to untangle herself from uncomfortable situations. Driving that ambulance was a big part of her life. The trouble was, Jarrett had been a big part of her life at one time, too. That didn't just make it a situation, that made it a crisis.

But she could handle it. She was older and wiser and more prepared. She would deal with it the way she dealt with crises when she drove the ambulance— calmly and efficiently.

She changed into jeans and a T-shirt for comfort and settled down with a cup of coffee. It was then she noticed the message light blinking on the answering machine. Pressing the button, she bit into one of the stale cookies she dug out of the cookie jar. The first call was from Matt reminding her about the dinner-dance on Friday night capping off the month-long fund-raiser. The second was from her Aunt Judy reminding her to respond to the baby shower invitation. Grumbling a bit, she made a note to do that. Then she heard Jarrett's voice and forgot everything else.

". . . if you get in before seven . . ."

Jessie looked at her watch. Too late. Even if she called the hospital right this second, she probably would have missed him. Cupping her chin with her hand, she listened to his voice.

"... looks like Sandy's going to make it. I just wanted you to know. Good night."

She rewound the tape and listened to it again. His voice was low and edged with control, but it wrapped around her: warm, familiar, and oddly physical. Calling herself a fool, she rewound it a second time, and then a third. Maybe she should give him a chance. He had come all this way to find something. He said it was her, but she sensed she wasn't the whole reason. If she kept him at arm's length, how would she ever know for sure?

In the morning she would stop by the bakery and buy some of those little chocolate cookies he always liked. And she'd make some cappuccino. What was the flavor he used to like? French vanilla?

Rising, she turned off the light and headed for the bedroom. Her T-shirt was half over her head when a knock interrupted her.

"Coming," she said, pulling her shirt back down and running her fingers through her hair. "Who is it?"

"Want three guesses again?" a familiar voice answered.

Jessie removed the security chain and opened the door. Jarrett stood there in jeans and a Mets jersey. He was balancing a bat on his left shoulder and tossing a baseball up and down with his right hand.

Grinning, he caught the ball and held it out to her. "Thought you might like to hit a couple in the batting cage for old times' sake."

Jessie blinked and wondered if she was seeing things. "This late at night? The cages are closed."

He pulled a set of keys from his back pocket. "Not to someone who plans ahead," he said with a smile as he twirled the ring around his forefinger. He noticed her hesitate. "Bad idea. You've probably forgotten how to take a decent cut at a fast ball."

"You're wrong about that."

"Prove it." He held the bat out to her.

She snatched it from his hand. "You're on."

Chapter Five

"**I** got your message about Sandy. I'm so relieved that she's going to be okay," Jessie said, walking with Jarrett to the batting cages located in a park a few blocks away.

"She's scared and confused, but she'll be around to celebrate her sixth birthday this weekend."

"Yes!" Jessie shouted. There was a flash, like light crossing water, when her gaze met his. "Thanks."

He squeezed her arm. "Thanks to you too. You got her to the ER quickly and gave her the edge she needed." He smiled, remembering. "But I'm not all that surprised. If I recall correctly, you never did anything halfway."

"Compliment or critique?" she asked.

Memories opened before him like a curtain being ripped aside. On the stage inside his mind, he replayed the last time he saw her before he went off to medical school. She was filled with determination and pride, ready to step out and make her mark on the world. Like a long-distance runner just hitting her stride, she had the drive and demeanor to succeed. Even if she hadn't known it yet, he had. He knew almost from that day in the chapel at her aunt's wedding when she snatched the baseball card from his hand and refused to give it back. She was energetic, dynamic, and neutral in nothing.

He had been right to let her go when he went off to medical school. She would never have been happy taking a backseat to his career. As painful as it was and still might be, everything turned out the way it had to be, even to the point of bringing them back together now.

"It was a compliment." He smiled.

"Thanks." Jessie smiled back. "Tell me, were you Chief of Emergency Medicine back east?"

He picked up a stone from the ground and threw it hard into the vacant lot they were passing. "No. This is new for me."

A car sped by as they walked and Jarrett moved to the outside, settling Jessie comfortably against his side. He slipped an arm around her waist. She didn't move away from it.

"Think you'll like it here?" she asked.

"So far I do." He kicked at another rock and sent it skipping into the street. "I like being able to help out in all the specialties and not limit myself to just one."

"Good thing this isn't New York, then. I hear big city hospitals don't like freelancing."

"You're right about that. There it's all categorized and sanitized. If you step out of your metier, you step on some pretty big toes in the process."

"Is that what you did?"

He pressed his lips together. He hoped the uneasiness didn't show in his eyes. "Let's just say I stubbed a few toes in my time. But then again, don't we all, Miss Payment Schedule?"

Jessie laughed. "Guess so."

"I was afraid that you might be asleep when I showed up on your doorstep," he continued.

"For the second time," she reminded him.

"It worked so well the first time, I figured, what the heck, I'm on a roll." Jarrett took a deep breath before speaking. "And as long as I am, it's time we settled up on a few things."

"I suppose it is," Jessie agreed, wishing she was wearing a thick jacket instead of a T-shirt. The way his fingers kept sliding up and down her back was distracting her. "To a certain extent at least."

"I was thinking that at first, but now I'm thinking something a little bit different."

"What's that?"

"I'm thinking how good you feel on my arm like this, and about how much I like being with you, talking to you. And I'm thinking, well, maybe we could work our way beyond what didn't happen to us and concentrate on what is happening now."

"Anything's possible, I guess. But I have a lot of things going right now. Like my job, my volunteer work, and the fundraiser. And you aren't really even settled in yet."

He kept on talking as though he hadn't heard her speak. "And I was thinking we should spend more time together."

"I'm not ready to . . ."

"Don't decide right now. I've waited this long to ask you. I can wait a little longer."

Jessie gave him a tight-lipped smile. She did want to see him more, but if she did, it would mean she would have to relive the past too. It had hurt so much the first time. She wasn't sure if she was ready to go through it again.

She started to respond but they turned the corner and the batting cages came into view, giving her an excuse to step out of Jarrett's embrace. "We're here."

"Let me get the place ready." He released the lock on the gate, swept it open and disappeared into the darkness. A moment later the area was bathed in bright yellow light from the overhead lights. In another second, the hum of machinery cut into the quiet of the evening.

Jarrett came back with two red batting helmets, each scratched and dented. He palmed one onto her head. "Ladies first. League rules."

She adjusted the helmet and headed for the cage. "How many practice swings do I get?"

"How many do you need?" he asked in a playful tone.

She tapped home plate with the bat and took her stance. "None."

"A little over-confident, aren't we?"

"Nope, just truthful."

"Okay. You're up."

Jarrett reached out and pressed the green button. The pitching machine whined and tossed out a ball at medium speed. Jessie took a full swing and knocked it to the back of the fence.

"That's one," she said, readying herself for the next pitch.

"Lucky shot," Jarrett countered.

Another swing, another fly ball to the rear of the cage. "Luck is not a factor here. It's talent, darlin', pure talent," Jessie said. "Tell you what." She stopped talking only long enough to send another ball to the fence with a hard swing and full contact of bat and ball. "You wanted to settle up. You can start right here."

"What do you mean?"

Another hard swing. Another hard hit. "Loser buys the hot dogs at the Sabrett wagon."

Jarrett slapped at the chain link fence with his palm. "You're on. You won't hit all twenty pitches."

Jessie gave him a sidelong glance. "Watch me, ace."

Ten singles later and Jarrett was beginning to get worried. She hadn't missed one. "Hey, aren't you afraid you might hurt yourself swinging that hard?"

Jessie didn't take her eyes off the ball as it came toward her or as it left her bat on its trip to the backstop. "Nope."

After the fifteenth straight hit he was really getting nervous. He'd have to break her concentration. When the ball left the pitching machine, he feigned alarm and shouted, "Watch out, it's coming at your head."

Jessie grinned. "I'll fix that." Another home run.

He tried another angle. "Isn't that Matt over there?" He motioned in the direction of the refreshment stand. "Hey, Matt, over here. C'mon, Jessie, don't be rude. Wave."

"He'll understand," she said right before she connected again.

He made one last-ditch attempt to get her to miss. "Arms feel okay? As your doctor I must warn you, strenuous exercise is best done in moderation."

"They're fine!" she called back as she hit the final pitch to the right.

Twenty pitches. Twenty hits. Jessie opened the door and flipped the bat in the air. She caught it at the thick end and handed it to Jarrett. "I believe my work here is done. Next batter."

"How many practice swings do I get?" Jarrett asked, taking his place in the box and sweeping the bat through the strike zone with a lazy loop.

"Same amount I had. None." She reached over and started the pitching machine. Soon the rhythmic crack of bat hitting ball filled the air.

Jessie had put everything she had into the first set and knew there was no way she could go through twenty more pitches and hit them all. Her arms ached and her hands stung. But she was not about to let Jarrett know it. She'd hit again, if she had to, even if it meant the heaviest thing she'd be able to pick up in the morning was her coffee cup. So far Jarrett had matched her hit for hit and, by her count, he had five pitches left. What she needed was a plan.

Or a diversion.

A sly little smile crept up on her lips. He had called her a distraction, hadn't he? Maybe it was time for her to live up to the name. She opened the batting cage to the right of the one Jarrett was using and stepped inside. Making sure he saw her, she pressed her right hip against the chain link fence and rattled it to get his attention.

She ran her hands through her hair. "Sure is warm out here for this time of year, don't you think?" Lacing her fingers together, she raised her hair from the back of her neck. "I'll just bet you didn't think the Midwest could be so warm."

Jarrett did a double take and then found himself mesmerized. In the golden glow of the overhead lights he watched her and became fascinated by the way she glowed in the reflected light. He leaned forward to get an even better look at her and the next pitch nearly hit him. He barely had time to whip his bat around and make weak contact.

As the ball bounced feebly past the pitching machine, Jessie knew she had his attention. "My, my, what power," she teased.

"It counts," he said quickly. "No one said how far the ball had to go after it was hit."

Jessie smiled. He was playing by her rules now. She adjusted the hem of her T-shirt. "Maybe the heat is affecting your game."

He watched Jessie in the adjoining batting cage and barely recovered his senses in time to knock the next pitch a paltry three feet in front of him.

Jessie put her hands on the fence and slid her palms along the metal links. "Uhmmm. This feels great; nice and cool. You should try it."

Jarrett tried to turn his attention back to the pitching machine, but he couldn't. He was sure Jessie could see the steam coming up from between the collar of his T-shirt and his neck because he could sure feel it. And if he were a betting man, he'd have bet she was enjoying every minute of this.

"No fair. Stop that," he said in a feeble protest as he managed to hit the next pitch more solidly.

"Stop what?" Jessie said in a voice that sounded like the tinkle of ice cubes in a glass of lemonade on a hot, summer day.

"You know darn well what I mean, woman," he said. He just barely nicked the next pitch with the bat.

"Why Dr. Collins, are you saying that I'm *distracting* you again?"

"Jessie . . ."

Last ball. She had to pull out all the stops now. As she heard the machine gear up for the final pitch, she grabbed the hem of her tee shirt and fanned it up and down. "That's better. Feels much cooler now." Her

voice was like honey as she ran her hands across her
bare midriff.

"That's it," he said as the last ball zipped past him
unnoticed, unoffered. A smile came to life on his lips.
"I can't do this anymore."

"Whatever do you mean?" she asked sweetly, still
playing her game. "Is there a problem?"

He tossed the bat to one side and stepped out of his
batting cage and into hers. As he walked toward her,
he locked his eyes on her face. He hooked his thumb
toward his chest and said, "I'm the problem because
right now I don't care about balls and bats and hitting.
All I care is about is getting over there and holding
you."

Jessie didn't resist when he reached her and
wrapped his arm around her shoulder. She found herself pressed against his light blue shirt, his chest a
pillow for her to rest her head against. When he ran
his fingers through her hair much like she had done,
she moved her head deeper into him and inhaled his
masculine scent laced with a hint of his woodsy cologne.

"That's much better," Jarrett whispered against her
ear. The need to kiss her was overwhelming, but he
held himself in check. He rested his jaw against her
silky hair and went on in a low, husky tone. "Now
you listen to me, Jessie. We're not kids anymore.
There's a price attached to everything we do now." He
inhaled her fragrance. "We aren't supposed to let situations get the best of us anymore." Giving her a little
shake, he reluctantly created a small space between
them and looked into her wide eyes. "I want to be
with you more than I've ever wanted anything in m'
life. Don't do anything like that again unless you wa'
to be with me too."

As Jessie eased away from him, her hand moved across his chest. She felt his muscles tense wherever she grazed him. She hadn't counted on this. In trying to teach him a lesson, she had created a situation in which there wouldn't be any winners. She forced herself to look into his eyes.

"Jarrett . . ." His name came out like a prayer. She pressed her hand against his chest and felt the urgent beating of his heart. "I'm sorry."

Gently, he released her. "I think I owe you a hot dog."

By the time they locked up the batting cages and got to the edge of the park, the hot dog cart was gone, so they settled for an ice cream cone instead. When they arrived back in the parking lot of Jessie's apartment complex, Jarrett sat on the hood of his car and Jessie leaned against the driver's door.

"You're dripping," he said. "The ice cream. It's about to run all over your hand."

Jessie tipped her hand. He was right. She was about to become chocolate-coated. The ice cream was dripping onto her knuckles. "Whoops. No napkins either."

Jarrett slid from the car hood and grabbed her hand. "Here, use mine."

Jessie pulled away. "Doctor Collins, the germs!" She feigned revulsion.

"You never complained about germs when we were kids. Remember at your aunt's wedding back when we were paired up as flower girl and ring bearer? We used the same fork to eat the cake."

"Well . . ." she hedged. She wished he wouldn't keep saying things that reminded her of the past. All the pleasant memories were winning the war against her sensibility. "We're adults now. There's a price attached to everything we do. Isn't that what you said?"

Jarrett swept his hand through the air. "Ka-bam!"

Caught off guard, Jessie jumped. "What was that?"

"The sound of the door between us slamming shut again," he said, pulling in a jerky sigh and wiping his hands on the sides of his jeans. "I wish you would open it back up. Just a little."

"Why?"

"So I could ask you something."

"Ask away."

"Why aren't you married?"

The question surprised her, and yet it didn't. She had been wondering when he was going to ask. She turned up her face to meet his eyes. Her gaze remained steady on his and the words spun inside her head. How could she tell him that she hadn't gotten married because she was waiting for him? A vague sensation of tension settled between her shoulder blades.

"Because I haven't found anyone that will put up with me on a steady basis yet," she replied, hoping her voice was convincing.

He hopped back up onto the hood of the car. "Ever get close?" he asked.

Jessie stared off into the distance. "I was kinda serious with a guy who wasn't very serious with me."

With a weak laugh Jarrett recognized the analogy. "He was a fool to let you go."

"Maybe he wasn't."

"Trust me. He was. I know the type. Intimately." He slid down and took her hand. "Listen. I'd better go. It's late and I have an early call in the morning." Somehow he resisted an overwhelming urge to drag her into his arms. "You swing a mean bat, Jessie O'Brien," he said with a laugh.

"You're welcome to a rematch any time."

"Promise?"

"Promise."

Jessie saw intensity come into his eyes as he leaned down toward her. His mouth looked so firm and strong. She knew he was going to kiss her. And she knew she wanted him to. Her breath caught in her throat as she felt his arms go around her. Jessie surrendered to his arms hearing her name whispered before their lips touched. She wrapped her arms around his neck and hung on for dear life.

After what seemed like an eternity, gradually, with eager, little kisses in between, they broke contact. Their breaths mingled as they stood, foreheads pressed together, looking into each other's eyes.

"I like what I see in your eyes," he said, caressing her hair and placing a kiss on her cheek.

Heart still hammering in her chest, Jessie lifted her eyes to his. "I'm not sure I'm ready for you yet," she admitted.

He knew she was right and he released her. "You've turned me down twice now. You know what they say: strike three and you're out." He smiled at her tenderly. "Good night, Jessie."

She wanted him to stay, but the warning voice in her head refused to be silent. She stepped back from his arms. "Good night, Jarrett."

She watched him leave until the taillights of his BMW became small dots in the dark night. Lost in a dream world of memories and kisses, she had no idea how long she stood there before turning and going inside.

Chapter Six

"You're not serious." Jessie looked up from the tuna sandwich she was eating at her desk and frowned.

Ann filled two plastic cups with diet soda and handed one to Jessie. "I am. Peggy says she has a date with the good doctor this Friday night."

"But that's the night of the fund-raiser dinner and I was going to ask him to go along as my guest," Jessie said with a sigh. *He wouldn't do that to me,* she thought.

"Then you should have asked him sooner." Ann mulled over her half-eaten sandwich. "Do you think Peggy's lying?"

"We'll just have to wait until Friday and see."

"Or you could ask him today and see what he says."

Jessie's eyes narrowed. "I can not. We're not dating. Jarrett's personal life is his business." Outside she remained calm, but inside she was shaking.

"You really didn't expect Peggy to stand back and

let that handsome doctor move out of her gun sights without at least taking a shot."

Jessie rolled her eyes. "Who can keep up with the woman? She was made for the chase."

"I hear you can."

"What?"

Ann smirked and leaned forward onto Jessie's desk with her forearm. "Rumor has it that you and Doctor Collins were seen conferring quite closely in the batting cages at Thompson Park last night."

Stunned that the news had traveled so quickly, Jessie grabbed onto the first passing thought to belie the guilt she was feeling. "We were just catching up on old times and hitting a few baseballs, that's all."

"Ida in legal says otherwise. She was on her way to the grocery store and was stopped at the light on Jefferson Street when you two caught her eye. The light turned green but . . . well, let's just say the light turned green a few times before she remembered to go."

Jessie felt her cheeks warm. "I suppose her version is all over the hospital already?"

Ann nodded. "Pretty much."

"Details, please."

Ann put the remnants of her lunch back into the small brown bag as she spoke. "Basically, Ida said that you two were all over each other, not caring who saw you."

Jessie groaned. Ida was the resident gossip, sort of like an echo chamber with feet. Everything she saw, heard, or thought she knew passed on to the first person who got in her sight line. In a small town like Tempest, gossip had been elevated to a career for someone like Ida.

"Well, she's wrong," Jessie said cautiously. "Anything else I should know?"

"Naw. About that time Peggy got her back up and started talking about Dr. Collins." Ann shifted on the chair. "Ida was pretty adamant about what she says she saw though."

Jessie said nothing, but felt a warm rush across her face, and knew that it was probably turning a vivid shade of red.

Ann looked Jessie up and down. "Shoulders tense, cheeks red, mouth tight—the body language is a dead giveaway."

"Okay, okay, we kissed," Jessie admitted, "but it wasn't racy or anything."

Ann snorted with laughter. "That's not what I heard."

"Get your dirty little mind out of the gutter," Jessie said with a chuckle of her own. "We have a whole lot of time to fill in and we were working on it a little at a time."

Ann propped an elbow onto the desk and leaned forward. "Just what were you working on last night? Ida said it was disgusting to watch."

Jessie breathed an exasperated sigh. "But not disgusting enough for her to drive away. What she thinks she saw, I don't know. It was a totally innocent kiss."

Ann shook her head. "I'm sorry to hear that."

Jessie pursed her lips. "You could try to sound a little more sincere."

"Next time call me so I don't have to listen to secondhand details."

"If there is ever anything worth telling, I will," Jessie said, glancing up at the clock on the wall opposite her desk. "Looks like lunch is over for me." She shot Ann a wry smile. "And just before you brought out the thumbscrews, too. Come on, I'll walk you to the elevator."

At the end of the hallway Ann pressed the down button on the elevator call panel. "Don't worry; if it's true about Peggy and Dr. Collins, Ida will be talking about them soon enough and the rumors about you will die a natural death."

Jessie was about to comment when the elevator doors opened and Jarrett stepped out. "Good afternoon, ladies."

"Dr. Collins." Ann acknowledged him with a nod as she exchanged places with him. Suddenly her hand shot out and stopped the door from closing. "Oh, Dr. Collins, a bit of advice," she said with a silly little grin, "watch out for the inside curve in cage four. I hear it's a killer." Her grin broke wide open just before the elevator doors closed.

"What was that all about?" Jarrett asked, as they turned and began to walk back to Jessie's office.

"Just some bad office humor," Jessie replied, in step beside him. "What brings you to my floor?"

"You."

With a one-cornered smile, Jessie forced herself to look up at him. "You are direct; I'll give you that."

He slung his chestnut-colored suit jacket over his right shoulder as they arrived at her office door. "I was hoping I could talk you into having lunch with me."

Jessie pointed to her desk, littered with used cellophane wrap, empty soda cans, and the packaging from her Oreos. "You're too late. I ate at my desk with Ann." She pointed to the clock. "I can't spare even another ten minutes right now." She smiled at him. What was it about a man with a jacket draped over his shoulder? He sure looked good. Posed like that, the bold lines of his upper body emphasized his broad shoulders, molded chest, and flat stomach.

"No problem," he replied with a grin. "You work, I'll watch." He tossed his jacket on a nearby chair and deposited himself on the corner of her desk. He fanned the air with his right hand. "Go on, get busy. Don't mind me."

Jessie realized right away that there was no way on earth she was going to be able to work with Jarrett so close to her. She watched him shuffle a few papers around on her desk and peek at some of the invoices that she was working on. His long fingers played with some paper clips, then the stapler, and then the pencil right in front of her. She watched, fascinated, as the movements rippled tendons and muscles in the back of his perfect hands. They were powerful, yet gentle enough to handle the most delicate precision surgical instrument with exactness. She looked back down to her ledger sheets and tried to center herself.

"Stop that," Jessie ordered, purposely not looking at him as she spoke.

"Stop what?" Jarrett asked, continuing to explore the desk, moving his hand closer and closer to hers.

"You know very well what," she countered. "If you're going to stay, and I'm sure that you are, then get off my desk, find a chair, and let me work." She looked up at him and was caught full force by the sunshine of his smile.

"Am I distracting you or something?" he asked, making no attempt to disguise the feigned innocence in his voice.

"You know very well that you are."

"Good. Now we're even." He slid from her desk and circled behind it to be near her. He pulled back the collar of her green silk blouse and put his hands on either side of her neck. Lightly he ran his fingers across the muscles of her shoulders. "Just as I thought. I can feel a real tenseness in this muscle group."

"You should. You put it there."

He smiled and pressed harder when he heard the erratic tone of her voice.

"Ow—not so hard."

"No pain, no gain," he replied, his fingers kneading the long muscles of her shoulders and back.

Jessie felt Jarrett's hands move in a caressing motion on her neck. She rolled her head one way, then the other, feeling the tension begin to release. It felt so wonderful that she didn't want him to stop, but she knew if anyone looked in from the hallway, the scene they saw would only fuel the gossip that was already galloping through the hospital like a runaway horse.

She lowered her chin to her chest, enjoying the rich sensation of his fingertips on her skin. This was heaven. "Hmm, that feels great, but you'd better stop."

"Why?" he asked, continuing the massage.

"Because if someone saw you doing that . . ."

"And saw you enjoying it."

". . . and saw me enjoying it, the story would be all over the hospital in no time. It's bad enough that everyone knows about last night."

Jarrett stopped massaging her neck and came around to the front of the desk. "What do they know about last night?"

Jessie paused for a moment, hesitant to give credence to the rumors by repeating them. "It seems as though everyone knows about batting practice."

"Nothing happened. Not that I wouldn't have liked it to." Jarrett raised his eyebrows up and down suggestively.

Jessie put down her pen and folded her arms across

her chest. "That's not the issue here. Do you know what happens in a small town like Tempest when one of the office biddies gets her teeth into some juicy gossip?"

The expression on Jarrett's face changed from playful to serious with the tone of her voice. "No, but in New York . . ."

She cut him off. "This is not New York."

"Jessie, why are you so angry with me? If someone is spreading rumors about you and me and last night, it certainly isn't me."

Jessie held up her hands. "Look, you just don't understand."

"Explain it to me then." He slid a chair next to her desk and sat down to face her. "I'm ready. Shoot."

Jessie gave him a long, level look. "Don't tempt me."

A smile crept up on his face. "A joke. There may be hope for this relationship after all."

"We don't have a relationship."

"We most certainly do," Jarrett insisted. He caught Jessie's hand in his own. "You might not be ready to admit it yet, but we do." He traced the outline of her hand with his forefinger. "I've missed you so much through the years, Jess. I tried hard not to, but I couldn't outrun the memories." He looked up into her eyes. "And now I don't want to outrun them. I want them back."

He stood and stepped forward with the urge to hold her. He shouldn't, he thought, not here. She was right. If anyone saw them, it would only generate more idle talk. But he couldn't stop himself. He leaned across her desk. "C'mere," he whispered, when his lips were a breath away from her face.

Jessie looked down a moment. She knew what he

wanted. She wanted it too. When she looked back at him, a tender light came into his eyes. She saw his gaze travel over her face to settle on her lips. "What are you doing?" The question was a breathless murmur.

"I think I'm going to kiss you."

Jessie's heart lurched and her pulse skidded. Against her will she leaned closer to his lips. "We . . . we shouldn't."

"That's right, you shouldn't!" The voice that bellowed out behind them belonged to Gordon Burrows. His burly form filled the doorway, feet spread, hands on hips, in an angry, disapproving posture.

Jessie jumped to her feet and met his cool stare, feeling herself blush as she did. She looked back to Jarrett, who had already straightened and put on his jacket.

"Dr. Collins," Burrows said stiffly, "I thought I may have heard your page not more than a minute ago."

By the stern, forbidding look on Burrows' face, Jarrett sensed that Jessie was in for a rough ride. They stood like a pair of marble statues, each waiting for the other to say something.

"Want me to stay?" Jarrett finally asked.

She held up an absolving hand. "No, if you were paged, it could be an emergency. You'd better check on it."

He dipped his head. "Are you sure?"

She nodded.

"I'll see you later then?"

She nodded again.

Burrows strode across the floor toward his office. "Miss O'Brien, I need the Harper file."

She nodded a third time, but did not move until his office door closed.

"Sorry, Jess," Jarrett said. "I didn't mean to get you in hot water with the boss."

Jessie picked up a thick folder and tucked it under her arm. "Try to keep your hormones under control in my office at least." She shoved the remaining papers on her desk into a pile. "Mostly Gordon's all bark and no bite. He probably had the chili downstairs in the coffee shop and now his ulcer is talking to him." She started toward his office. "Better answer that page."

Jarrett winked and hurried off.

Just outside the door, Jessie took a deep breath, turned the knob, and then pushed the door open with her hip. "Here's the file you wanted," she said brightly, walking to his desk and depositing it in front of him. "Will there be anything else?"

Gordon nodded toward the empty chair next to her. "Yes. Sit down." Once she was seated, he shook his head in a gesture that signaled his disappointment. "Exactly what were you doing out there?"

"Nothing," she answered quickly.

"Nothing?" He snorted. "I was young once. That nothing was about to be something if I hadn't walked in."

"I had the situation under control."

He ignored her feeble protest and snorted his disapproval. "I could see that." He paused as though he was trying to gather his thoughts. "Jessie, do you know that the whole hospital is talking about you two?"

"Ann told me. But my relationship with Dr. Collins is not anyone's business but our own."

"On the contrary," Gordon countered, "you're forgetting that you're in line for my job when I retire at the end of the year. I suspect that the Board of Trustees will not look too kindly on someone whose reputation is less than stellar. You know how uppity they can be."

Jessie waved off the notion. "Oh for heaven's sake. You talk like this place is 'General Hospital' or something." She pressed a hand to her forehead. All this preoccupation with her personal life was building a headache behind her eyes.

"Is it?" he asked suddenly.

For a moment everything turned red in front of Jessie's eyes. There was no talking to him about this, to anyone for that matter. Apparently everyone had already drawn their own conclusions about what was or wasn't going on between her and Jarrett. She might as well be wearing a scarlet 'A' on her chest.

She clamped her jaw. "Mr. Burrows." She saw his eyes widen and his body tense. She only called him that when she was ready to fight and he knew it. "If I'm mature and intelligent enough to be considered by the Board for your job, then I think I'm mature and intelligent enough to handle things when I'm not on the job."

"And you choose to handle it by airing your personal life in a public place?"

Jessie's shoulders dropped. "Gordon, I told you, nothing has happened." She narrowed her eyes. "Tell me, as a professional and financial advisor, do you invest money for Midwest Medical on hearsay, or do you investigate all the options before coming to a conclusion?"

Gordon shrank back from her counter. "One situation has nothing to do with the other."

"Oh, but they do. Just because someone tells you something, doesn't make what's being said the gospel truth." She wagged her finger in the air at him. "Always check the facts. I believe you were the one to tell me that." She studied him levelly before asking, "And I've lived in this town long enough to know how it operates. So give me a little credit."

Burrows dropped his shoulders. "Jessie, I just don't want you ruining your career and your future because of a . . . oh, there's no delicate way to put this . . . because of a man." He looked her squarely in the eyes. "You do know why Dr. Collins came to Tempest, don't you?"

"I think so," she said in a voice that she knew told Gordon otherwise.

He rose and walked around the desk. Taking her arm, he gently pulled her to a standing position and walked her to his office door. "I'm no gossip, so maybe you had better ask him. Just to be sure."

Jessie felt the warmth drain from her. Was there something else Jarrett hadn't told her?

Chapter Seven

J essie was still thinking about Jarrett when she got out of the elevator on 3-West, the hospital's Physical Medicine and Rehabilitation wing. She shifted the teddy bear she was carrying into the crook of her left arm and began to walk down the hallway. She scanned the numbers as she passed each room until she found 382.

Inside on the bed closest to the window lay Sandy Wilson. Her head turned toward the door when Jessie entered. Sandy's mother was sitting on a chair next to the bed holding her hand.

Jessie walked to them and smiled. "Hello, Sandy. My name is Jessica. How are you feeling?" Sandy's wide, doubting eyes only stared.

Sandy's mother swept back a lock of unruly hair that had fallen out of the top of the thick bandage wrapped around the little girl's head. "Honey," she said, "this is the lady I told you about, the one who gave you a ride here in her ambulance."

"Can I sit down for a minute, Sandy?" Jessie asked.

Sandy nodded glumly.

Jessie pulled over the worn gray metal chair and placed it next to the bed. "Sandy. That's a real nice name."

"It's not my real name," the little girl said. "My real name is Cassandra."

"That's a lovely name. Do your friends call you Sandy?"

She nodded.

"My friends call me Jessie."

Sandy looked at the teddy bear nestled in the crook of Jessie's arm. "Is that for me?"

"Sure is." She placed the teddy bear on the bed. "His name is . . ."

"Doctor Jarrett," Sandy said, finishing the sentence. She nestled the bear next to her in bed.

"That's a very unusual name for a teddy bear," Jessie said in an interested voice.

"Sandy has taken a liking to Dr. Collins," Mrs. Wilson explained. "And fortunately Dr. Collins doesn't seem to mind. He's the only one who can get Sandy to cooperate during her therapy sessions."

"Is that right?" Jessie mused.

"Dr. Jarrett fixed my head," Sandy said. "If he didn't sew it up, all my brains would have fallen out the hole that got in it when Mommy and I had our accident."

"Did Dr. Jarrett tell you that?"

"Nope, I just knew it."

Jessie smiled at the simplicity and innocence in the little girl's statement. Apparently no one told her that

Jarrett also helped to save her life. Sandy's parents would most likely explain everything to her when she was stronger and ready to understand. For now, it was enough for her to think that he merely tucked everything safely back inside her head where it belonged.

"Well, I think Dr. Jarrett is pretty special for doing that," Jessie said, rising from the chair.

"He is." Sandy adjusted her position and pulled the covers up to the teddy bear's chin.

"And you should keep listening to what he says. If you do, pretty soon you'll be able to see your friends at school again."

Sandy's eyes brightened. "I know. When I go back, maybe I could bring Dr. Jarrett in for Show and Tell. He could bring his doctor stuff and show the class what he used to put my brains back in." Her voice rose in excitement. "I hafta ask him what it was. I bet it was a spoon or something. Kinda like the one Mom uses for spaghetti sauce."

In spite of the strange picture Sandy was painting, Jessie laughed along with Sandy's mother. "Now that's something I'd like to see too. But for now, I think you need to get some rest." She stood up and patted the bear's furry head. "You take real good care of Dr. Jarrett now."

Sandy smiled broadly. "I will."

"I'll walk you to the door," Mrs. Wilson said.

"'Bye Sandy," Jessie said. "Can I come back and see you?"

"Sure, but I'm going home soon." Suddenly her eyes brightened. "I know; you can come to my birthday party. It's on Friday. After dinner."

Jessie smiled. "I'd love to, but I've already promised to help some people raise money to buy a new ambulance."

"Better than the one I rode in?"

"Much better."

"So it can help you bring other kids here so Dr. Jarrett can help them."

"That's right."

Sandy hunkered down under the covers and yawned. "Okay, then. But maybe you can come after."

"I'll try." Jessie reached over and tucked in the blanket around Sandy and her bear. "You rest now. I think Dr. Jarrett is sleepy, too."

Sandy pulled the bear closer to her. " 'Kay."

Mrs. Wilson and Jessie walked together to the door. "Sandy sure perked up after naming her teddy bear," Jessie said.

"Just the mention of Dr. Jarrett does that to her. He has a way of making her smile when no one else can. Do you know he stops by here almost every morning to check on her and then comes back around two o'clock to walk Sandy to therapy?"

"Does he?"

"Yes, and then every night, he comes by just to say good night. Dr. Collins is a very special man to do all that."

"Yes, he is," Jessie agreed. Being around him again, she was beginning to realize just how extraordinary he was.

In the hallway, out of earshot of her daughter, Mrs. Wilson's voice took on a more serious tone. "I just want to thank you again for all you've done for us," she said. "If it wasn't for you and Dr. Collins . . ." She paused, her eyes filling with tears.

Jessie reached out and touched her arm. "Don't think about that. Think about all the wonderful years you're going to have with Sandy."

"And Dr. Jarrett, the bear."

"Him, too."

Mrs. Wilson took a step back inside. "I'd walk you to the elevators, but I don't want to leave her for too long."

"I don't blame you a bit."

She watched from the hall as Mrs. Wilson returned to her daughter's side. She couldn't tear her eyes from the scene. Mother and daughter shared a bond and an understanding that need not be put into words for each to know they were loved by the other. Mrs. Wilson lovingly stroked her daughter's head and Sandy held tightly onto mother's hand, both wrapped in the miracle that this display of love was able to take place at all. The thought made Jessie's eyes well up with tears.

Suddenly she began to feel it really wasn't all that important why Jarrett had come to Tempest. The only thing that mattered was that he came in time to save Sandy.

Elbows resting on her knees, Jessie sat cross-legged in front of the sofa, looking at the well-aged cigar box on the floor in front of her. It was a nondescript container, edges worn, top peeling, but it could not have been more precious to her if it were made of gold. Inside it was her past, and possibly her future.

She picked up the box with her forefingers and thumbs and held it as though it were one of those old-fashioned, fragile Easter eggs, the kind with the yolk blown out from tiny holes at each end. Taking a deep breath, she flipped open the lid with the tip of her right index finger. Her Pandora's box didn't explode, but it did detonate a storm of memories.

On top were some old letters. She recognized Jarrett's elementary school scrawl and smiled with memory. He hated to write, but he managed to get off at least one letter a month to her in handwriting that seemed more like aimless scribbling than organized English. It was an early sign of his eventual rise to the medical profession, she guessed.

She dug deeper. There were a few birthday cards, a tag from an old Christmas package and a postcard from Disney World. She ran her fingertips across an out-of-focus picture Jarrett had taken of his cat, Sneakers. He had earmarked the day he took the photo as a monumental occasion: he and the cat were both ten years old.

All nice memories, but none the one she was looking for. She rummaged through other papers and mementos, getting a little nervous when she saw the tan-colored bottom of the box peeking out from underneath the rest of the items. It was here somewhere. She knew it. She didn't remember ever taking it out.

And then, finally, there it was, at the bottom, right where she had put it over twenty years before: the baseball card.

She took it from the box and put it in the palm of her right hand. Could it really have been that many years since she snatched it out from under Jarrett's nose in the vestibule of the church, signaling the beginning of their relationship?

It wasn't that he hadn't earned the card back by his good behavior that day. He had. She had just forgotten to give it to him after the wedding and then never got around to returning it once she got home to Wisconsin. He asked for it regularly for a while, and she always meant to mail it back, but somehow she always got sidetracked and forgot to send it. He asked less frequently as he got older, until he stopped mentioning it altogether. Eventually she forgot about it too. In fact, she had forgotten about the box until her Aunt Judy sent it to her only last year after finding it in the back of her closet during spring-cleaning at Grandma Ginger's house.

She tapped the card on her chin. She thought about a variation on that line from *Casablanca*: Of all the hospitals, in all the small towns, in all the world, why did he come walking into hers?

He said it was because of her, because of what they had in the past. That might have been part of it, but she was almost sure it wasn't the whole reason. Jarrett wouldn't have told Burrows that he came to Tempest because of her; it was much too personal a revelation for polite conversation. There had to be something else.

Obviously they had feelings for each other. But she wished she had been more prepared for his entrance back into her life. He'd caught her off balance—off stride—and she hadn't had time to completely recover. It didn't help being around him so much, either. It was getting harder and harder for her to keep her senses in check. She wasn't quite sure that she really wanted to anyway; he felt too good in her arms. She had to decide what to do about him before their relationship went any further. And it was going to go further. She was sure about that.

A knock at the door sent her scurrying to put everything back inside the box. She slipped it under the sofa. These were her private, precious memories. She had only recently gotten them back and she didn't want to share them with anyone yet.

She placed her hand on the door. "Who is it?"

"Your friendly neighborhood doctor."

She yanked open the door. "Hi."

He held out a bunch of roses in an array of beautiful colors ranging from a deep red that looked like fine wine, to a soft pink that could only be found on the cheeks of sleeping babies, to the kind of white you would expect to find on the wings of an angel. "For you," he said. "I picked them myself."

Jessie furrowed her brow. The only place she'd seen roses like this was in the prize-winning flowerbed that belonged to the superintendent's wife. "Where did you get these?" she asked suspiciously, reaching out but then stopping right before she would take them from his hands.

Jarrett cocked his left thumb over his shoulder. "Around the corner and in front. There's a whole bunch of them."

Jessie grabbed his outstretched arm and pulled him inside. "Get in here before the superintendent sees you and gives me an eviction notice."

He studied her for a moment, then a grin lifted one corner of his lips. "They're his?"

"His wife's. And she's been known to prosecute poachers." Jessie stuck her head out the door and looked up and down the street. "You're safe for the moment. Not a person in sight."

Jarrett lifted his shoulders. "I saw them and remembered how much fun we used to have raiding gardens to pick flowers for your Aunt Judy whenever you were visiting her back east."

Jessie took the flowers and walked into the kitchen. "To tell you the truth, I've been dying to get my hands on a red one, but I didn't have the nerve to pick one." She pulled the dark-colored rose from the middle of the bunch. "It looks so velvety soft. Do you know what I mean, when something looks so soft that you just have to touch it?" She looked up to find Jarrett staring at her.

"I most certainly do."

"You're impossible." She giggled.

"But likeable, right?"

"So far." She ran some water into a vase and began to arrange the roses. "So why flowers? It's not my birthday."

"November 23. That's your birthday."

"You have a good memory, Doctor." She smiled. "I thought you'd forgotten. I hadn't gotten a card from you since I was . . . well, let's just say it's been a while. What's the occasion?"

"A peace offering. For the scene in your office." He laughed ruefully. "I acted like an idiot. I swear it won't happen again. Sometimes I forget where I am."

"It's okay." She saw him look pensively at her. "Honest. No real harm done."

"You're sure?" His voice was soft, as though his world had just been righted.

"Positive." She stopped, remembering what Ann had said. "A few days and there'll be something else to occupy the gossips." She wondered if she should ask Jarrett if he had a date with Peggy, but the look on his face, a mixture of uneasiness and determination, made her think better of it.

He picked up the vase from the sink. "Where's the perfect spot for these flowers?"

"I know." Jessie took the roses from him. He watched her walk away into the living room, her slim hips, tucked neatly inside the jeans she was wearing, moving with a slight sway. Though not quite as tight as the jeans she used to wear when they were kids, these looked pretty good on her, too. When they rounded softly around her hips as she bent down to put the vase on an end table, his bones seemed to turn to mush.

"There. Perfect," she said, spinning around quickly

and crossing her arms in front of her chest. "Now that we've gotten the matter of the roses and their place in this universe out of the way, you can tell me what's wrong."

"What do you mean?" He took a few steps closer to her.

Buoyed by the memories inside the cigar box, Jessie knew right away something was on his mind. "We may have been apart for the past few years, but I still recognize the routine." She circled him as she spoke. "Flip attitude, big smile, funny jokes. Yep, you have all the symptoms, Doctor. Something's bothering you."

He took her hand as they sat on the sofa. "That obvious?"

"Only to the trained eye." His touch sent shivers up her spine and raised the fine hairs on her arm.

"I didn't mean to come into your life like a commando and put so much pressure on you, Jessie." He threw his head back and blew out a long breath of air. "I want to clear the air between us, but so much has happened."

"Is it that serious, Jarrett?"

He remained silent for a long time, staring at the stack of magazines on the coffee table. "It could be."

"Then maybe you should tell me."

"I know I should." His voice betrayed his apprehension. "Remember how we used to dream about building a house in Florida someday?"

"Yes, I remember, but that was years ago."

He went on as though she hadn't spoken. "We said we wanted it near the Magic Kingdom so we could go to the castle any time we wanted to. Then we'd ride the Skyway Ride from one end of the park to the other to see if we could see the house." He leaned forward and rested his elbows on his thighs. "It was going to be a big house with lots of windows and natural wood. The master bedroom was going to be huge with closets made of cedar and a deck with a view overlooking a small lake." He spoke in an odd tone filled with quiet emphasis. "And we'd have four bedrooms, one for us, one for the twins, the others for their brother and sister." He reached into his shirt pocket, pulled out a photograph, and handed it to her.

Jessie's heart pounded as she took it. Her lips dropped open and her eyes widened when she looked at it. The picture showed a house built near the edge of a small lake. More than that, it showed their house. It was the house she and Jarrett had made up in letters, over the phone, in notes and cards, and in secret whisperings in the dark almost a decade ago. From its appearance, he had remembered everything they said and brought it to life. She looked at him, waiting for an explanation. For a while, he had none to give her.

His hoarse whisper broke the silence. "I built it for you."

"No you didn't," she returned sharply.

He heard the disbelief in her voice and saw her expression grow serious. "I have to know, what are you thinking?"

"Oh, Jarrett." Her voice shook. "You built this house, our house, and you built it for someone else."

A thick stillness seemed to settle around them. Jarrett shifted uneasily. "I didn't set out to build our house. I simply wanted a place I could escape to when the pressure started weighing me down—to lose myself for a while. So I started with an empty lot and just kept going. It wasn't until the house was finished and I was walking through it one day that I realized what I had done." He kept his features composed when he added, "And then I was glad that I had. It felt right and warm and safe." He turned around to look directly at her. "It felt like home."

Jessie tore her gaze from his face and studied the pattern on the sofa. "I . . . I don't know what to say."

"Don't say anything. I just wanted to you know."

"Why?"

"Guilt, I suppose."

"And you used me to purge it?"

"That wasn't the intent."

Their eyes met and she saw vulnerability within the man. The doctor who always had to be so carefully in control was losing his edge. She looked at the photo again. "Your wife. Does she live there now?" It hurt her to acknowledge that another woman had won his heart.

He shook his head and dipped his chin. "No. I had to sell it as part of the divorce settlement. After she made it a pawn, I didn't want it anyway." When he looked back at Jessie she was staring at the picture, her brow furrowed, her face pained. He took the photo from her and ripped it in two. He let the portions fall from his hand and watched them flutter to the carpet. "I wanted a new beginning, but I don't know how to do it right."

Jessie slid from the sofa, sat down on her heels, and picked up the pieces. She matched the edges together and looked at the house for a long moment before she put them back into his hand. "You're doing fine. I was just a little stunned, that's all. Keeping this secret inside would have been much worse as time went on." She curled his fingers around them. "Now you can let it go." Deep inside her she knew it was right for her to forgive him. It was the only way they could both go on.

Their eyes met and held. Jessie felt a rich sense of closeness to him. He was finally beginning to open up to her and talk about the years when they were apart. Slowly, one step at a time, it was happening.

"Does this mean you aren't going to toss me out on my ear?" he asked.

Jessie could see the tension easing in his eyes. She shook her head.

A grin tugged at his lips. "Is there anything I can do right now to make it up to you?"

"Yes," she blurted out without much thought. "Break your date for Friday night."

"Word does get around this town quickly," he said with a slanting grin.

"So it is true then."

"Yep, she was quite persistent."

A pain squeezed her heart when she thought of Jarrett with Peggy. "The squad is having a fund-raiser and I was hoping that you would go with me," she said with rising dismay.

Jarrett's smile vanished. "Sorry, sweetheart, but I gave my word. I hope you understand that I just can't disappoint her."

Jessie couldn't believe her ears. Apparently Peggy's blatant flirting had made a much greater impact on Jarrett than she had imagined. "No I don't understand." She made no attempt to disguise her annoyance. "I thought we were . . . well, getting close to each other again."

"I thought so, too." He hesitated, blinking in bafflement. Jessie's face was set, her expression pained. Her lips were drawn into a tight line. "What's wrong?"

"Nothing." She dropped her lashes. "I guess we can't disappoint Peggy, can we?" She heard the bitterness spill over in her voice.

"What has Peggy got to do with this? I thought we were talking about Friday night."

"We are."

"Maybe I am, but you're not. The lady I'm seeing this weekend is Miss Cassandra Wilson, not Nurse Peggy."

Jessie stared at him and then burst out laughing. She felt her cheeks warm with a blush, more embarrassed by how happy she felt being wrong, than she was by the confusion. "It's Sandy?"

He nodded. "Yep, Sandy. It's her birthday, and I promised I'd come to her party."

She put a hand to her mouth and blew out a breath of air that whistled through the spaces between her fingers. "I'm so embarrassed."

"Well, I'm flattered." He didn't just smile, he beamed. "You were jealous."

"I was not."

"Were too. I saw it all over your face."

"Okay, maybe a little. But who can compete with that little doll? She has those enormous brown eyes and that beautiful jet black hair down past her shoulders."

"From where I sit, you can."

With genuine effort, Jessie ignored the compliment. "I can understand not disappointing her. She certainly does seem to like Dr. Jarrett."

"Which one? Fur or flesh?"

"You know?"

He shifted his body and placed his right ankle on his knee before hooking an arm over the back of the sofa. "She couldn't wait to show me the teddy bear when I checked on her before I left the hospital. She told me the lady who gave her a ride to the hospital gave it to her. That was really sweet of you."

"She gave me quite a scare in the ambulance," Jessie said seriously. "I thought she wasn't going to make it." She struggled to control the panic she felt rising just thinking about that day. "I promised myself that no one would ever die in my ambulance. I thought she was going to be the first."

He sat up straight and leaned forward, forearms on his knees. "You shouldn't make that promise, Jessie." He closed his eyes for a fraction of a second to control the memory forcing its way into his brain. "It's too hard to keep."

"I know. But I just want to make a difference."

"You do. Sandy will probably be released on Monday."

"Thanks to you, I hear. Her mother told me that you're the only one who can get her to do her therapy."

"Mrs. Wilson exaggerated. It really wasn't that hard to get Sandy to cooperate. She just needed some coaxing. Anyone could have done it."

"But you did."

She watched him blush, and thought about his kindness to Sandy. As she did, she became aware of an emptiness that was being filled now that Jarrett was here with her. Caught in a web of her own weaving, she knew with pulse-pounding certainty that it was only a matter of time before she admitted to herself that he was right to come for her, and that it would be right for her to go wherever he would take her.

She straightened to her knees and ran a finger across his cheekbones. "I have to admit, red looks good on you."

He put a hand to his face and found that it was warm. "Must be getting a fever."

"I don't think so." She put her hand over his. "It's

something else. Mrs. Wilson told me all the trouble you go through for Sandy."

Their eyes met and caught. "Maybe I should be a pediatrician," he said quietly. "I love kids."

"After all those years of marriage, I'm surprised you don't have some." She saw his cheek twitch in reaction.

"It wasn't in the cards."

Jessie noticed an edge of despair in his voice. She bit down on her bottom lip, knowing that what she was about to ask might only add to his angst. "Jarrett, I know this might not be the best time, but there's something I need to know."

He studied her with curious intensity and noted the abrupt change on her face. "Now who's so serious?" Her eyes were pools of uncertainty. "Ask away, honey."

"Gordon asked me if I knew why you came to Tempest. I told him that I did, but I don't think I really know the whole story." Her voice took on an almost apologetic tone. "I'm sorry, but I have to ask. Did you really come to Tempest because of me, or were you running from your divorce?"

Jarrett let his shoulders wilt and hoped his answer wouldn't push Jessie over the line. "I've been thinking about that myself lately."

"And what have you decided?"

"That it may have been a little because of my screwed-up marriage, but it was a lot because of you." He felt himself panic now that the words were out. "I didn't lie that day in the emergency room when I first saw you again, Jessie—honest. You have to believe that."

"I'd like to."

His fingers played with the gold bracelet on her

wrist. "When I realized that my wife was just using me as a stepping stone, I felt disconnected to everyone and everything around me."

"What do you mean by stepping stone?"

"Angie, my ex, was model perfect. Never a hair out of place, perfect designer clothes, nails done every week."

Jessie looked down at her hands. "I have keyboard nails. Banging away at the computer makes me keep them short."

Jarrett grinned. "I have no problem with that. I don't care about the packaging. It's what's inside that counts."

"Maybe you should have opened the package before you took it home," Jessie said candidly.

"I know I should have. I was foolish and got caught up in the illusion. The real woman came out of that pretty box about six months after we got married and by then I was trapped."

"Trapped? How?"

"Angie handpicked me out of all the med students so she could have the same life her parents had. She had it all planned; I'd intern at Johns Hopkins, do my residency in Europe somewhere, and then slide into a management position at the medical school. We'd be seen with all the right people, do the political scene, and vacation for three months a year on the Riviera."

Jessie felt the expression on her face close. "When would you have time to practice medicine?"

He looked her square in the eyes. "Never. And no time for children either." He swallowed hard. "But I'm not a quitter, so I tried; I really tried. My life began to spin out of control, farther and farther away from the future I'd always envisioned, until I finally realized why." He looked deeply into Jessie's eyes. "It was time to admit my life had taken an abrupt wrong turn when I turned away from you. I had to find you, Jess, even if you tossed me out on my ear. I had to make sure you were happy before I could begin to find some happiness of my own."

"And suppose I had been married with six kids?"

He lowered his eyes and then quickly raised them to gaze at her face. "I would have wished you well, closed the book on us, and never bothered you again." He ran a finger down her cheek and across her lips. "But it didn't happen that way, and I believe it's because we're destined to be together."

"If you thought that, why didn't you tell me this earlier?"

"I meant to, a million times. But every time I got up the courage, I'd flounder and tell myself another time would be better. It seemed as though everyone I'd ever loved, I managed to hurt somehow, and I knew I was going to hurt you again by emptying my excess baggage at your feet. We've been apart so long that I wasn't sure you would understand. Sometimes I don't even understand myself what I did and why."

"We all make mistakes, Jarrett. I may not truly understand why you had to run off and get married, but I know firsthand that our own plans and dreams can take a few twists and turns. We're not perfect. We make choices and then have to make the best of what we're given next."

"I know that now." He was in grave danger of tearing down the shaky web of trust he was so painstakingly building over the last few days and he knew it. He inclined his head. "How much of a mess have I made?"

Jessie reached up and cupped his jaw with her hand. "I honestly don't know. I won't lie to you. Your leaving me was a huge hurt. It took me a long time to get over you."

"Then you're a stronger person than I am because I never got over you."

Jessie inhaled sharply and let her hand fall from his cheek. "You've given me so much to think about." His eyes told her that he understood.

He took her hand in his and kissed her palm. "You're good for me, Jessie. I only wish I could convince you that I'm good for you."

"We have to go slow at this and be sure." She removed her hand from his face, took his hand, and twisted their fingers together. For a while he seemed content just to sit there and stare at her. When she couldn't stand it any longer she asked, "What are you looking at?"

"You." He grinned more broadly. "I'm trying to get used to the fact that I'm with you again."

"Oh are you now?" She let him massage the back of her knuckles with his thumb. "Just because I said we're going to take this slow, doesn't mean we're going to end up together."

He ignored her comment. "Come here, Jessie," he said. He drew her to him and slipped to the floor. Once there, he pushed the table away with one hand and pulled her closer with the other. He kissed her lips, her cheeks, her forehead. Then he drew away and knelt there, facing her, not knowing what to do next to convince her that she was meant for him.

He tucked a strand of blond hair behind her ear. "You were saying?"

"I forget," she whispered. It was difficult for her to think, the way her pulse was racing.

He took her hands, and together they sat back on

the couch. "Good. Let's neck until you remember what it was."

She laughed nervously. "You're still impossible."

He caressed her face with such a light touch that it could scarcely be discerned. As he continued to trace the contour of her face with tender contact, he watched her eyelids drift shut and felt her move closer to him.

"I don't know what you expect from me," she whispered, with a sigh that was somewhere between resistance and surrender. "I don't know what I expect from myself." With a gentle yet firm nudge, she eased him away.

He again traced the line of her jaw with his forefinger. "Jessie, what are you afraid of?"

She reached for his hand and moved it from her face. "Honestly? I'm afraid of it all. You, me, the past repeating itself." She looked away, hoping she would be able to think more clearly if she wasn't lost in his eyes. "I want to know what happened to us and why, but as each little bit gets revealed, it makes me more confused than ever."

Jarrett ran his tongue against the back of his teeth. He was moving too fast with her, telling her too much of the gruesome details before she was ready to handle them. "Showing you the house wasn't such a great idea, was it?"

Jessie tensed.

"You're afraid I'm using you," he said, hoping for the denial he was too intelligent to expect.

"That's part of it."

"And the other part?"

"Maybe I'm using you." She paused for a moment. "There are still feelings between us, it would be senseless to deny that. But sometimes I wonder why they're still there."

"Does it matter?"

"To me it does. Aren't you worried that maybe I expected too much from you when I was a teenager, and now I see a chance to turn the tables for a little revenge?"

"I'm willing to take that chance," he said, without hesitation. He took her hand and placed it on his chest so she could feel the strong, fast thud of his heart. "Feel that? It's what you do to me when we're together. When I'm not with you, it's as though my heart stops completely."

The longer she sat there with her hand over his thundering heart, the more willing she was becoming to take that chance too. "There's something else. Something that maybe is a little selfish on my part," she admitted. "People talk here in Tempest. They say all sorts of terrible things that other people take as gospel. I don't want to be put in the same class as Peggy." She sighed. "And it wouldn't be fair to you either if you were known as the Casanova from New York who came here and swept the poor country girl off her feet. Even though I—I . . ."

He spread his fingers across her cheek. "You what? Say it, Jessie."

"Say what? That maybe it wouldn't be too far from the truth?"

"Would it, Jess?"

Drawing a deep breath she began, her voice a barely audible whisper. "There are some things I just can't deny: that I find you more than I bargained for; that I want you hold me forever. But Jarrett, I don't want an affair. I want something permanent. Something that will last."

Jarrett nodded. He knew. Commitment and trust. The two should be intertwined. Unfortunately for him, those two very important emotions were not quite set together firmly enough for Jessie to ward off the inevitable 'what-ifs.' "I know that," he said quietly.

Jessie waited several moments for him to say more. When he didn't, she realized that he was still holding back. It was as though there was another side to his story that he was reluctant to tell her. Her voice was low, her emotions controlled. "And you can't give me something permanent right now, can you?"

He captured her hand and slouched back against the sofa cushion. "Your hard work and determination are two of the qualities I most admire in you."

"But . . ."

He looked down at their interlaced fingers. "I've heard you're in line for a well-deserved promotion. I'd be a fool to get in your way."

"Just a second." She pulled her hand away. "What are you talking about, getting in my way?"

"I don't know. A feeling I've been getting lately." He looked at her and waited until her gaze met his. "You owe it to yourself to take the job if the Board offers it to you."

"Of course I'd do that." She bit down on her lip to drive away the wayward thoughts.

He pulled her into his arms and held her close, her shoulders against his chest. His lips brushed her hair once, then twice, before he settled her head under his chin. "As hard as it is for me to admit, I'm finding my timing might not be right for you right now."

She looked straight ahead, the stinging feeling within consuming her. He wasn't ready. He still wasn't ready for something solid. But she couldn't let him go. Not again.

Jarrett read her silence as refusal. "Do you want me to leave?" he asked.

Jessie's heart leapt to her throat. Her nerves hummed in anticipation. "No," she whispered.

His eyes were drawn to her lips, so close that if he just moved an inch he could kiss her once again. "Listen, neither of us is thinking clearly right now. It's late and we're both vulnerable. That could be an explosive combination."

Jessie turned her body more fully to his and traced a fingertip across his lower lip. "I know," was all she could manage to whisper.

"I don't want to leave you tonight, Jessie. I can't face going home to an empty place."

Jessie dropped her eyes, caution and irresponsibility warring inside her heart. When she looked back up and into his eyes, she saw an appeal she could not refuse.

"The only thing I can offer you is the couch, Jarrett. Nothing more."

His smile was heartrending when he replied. "I'll take it."

Chapter Eight

The smell of fresh coffee hit her nose as she slid from the bed.

She went downstairs and headed for the kitchen. She could hear the crackle of bacon cooking on the stove and the banging sound of pots hitting the stainless steel sink. She stopped just inside the archway and leaned against the wall, still holding an afghan close to her body. The place was in shambles. Pots and dishes were piled in the sink. Butter was spread everywhere except on the toast that was on a plate on the kitchen table. There was not one spot on the countertop that didn't appear to be covered with some type of food.

"I thought doctors worried about cholesterol," she said, nodding toward the stove.

Jarrett turned from the sink, his mouth curling into a smile when he saw her. She looked great; blond hair tousled, eyes just brightening. More than once during the past ten years he had imagined what she would look like in the morning if they had ever gotten married. Now he knew. And now he wanted to see her like this every morning.

He walked over to her while stirring eggs in a glass mixing bowl with a wire whisk. "Did my banging around in here wake you?"

Jessie looked from the eggs to the butter to the frying pan loaded with sizzling bacon. "No, I heard your arteries clogging all the way upstairs."

Jarrett laughed and put the dish on the counter. "I know a good cardiologist in New York just for occasions like this. I hope you're hungry. I know I am."

She sat down at the table. It was set for breakfast, juice poured, butter nicely softening, and syrup ready. "You did all this? When did you learn to cook?"

"During my internship. When we pulled those forty-eight hour shifts, some of us used to sneak down to the kitchen and turn whatever was left over that day into a gourmet feast."

"You're full of surprises, aren't you?"

"You've just seen the beginning, lovely lady," Jarrett said as a strawberry pastry popped up from the toaster. He put it on a plate and held it out to her.

She shook her head. "I don't usually eat breakfast."

"I guess that's why you're so skinny."

"Excuse me?"

He put the plate in the sink and rubbed his stomach with his palms. "Those hip bones of yours could be deadly weapons."

"I didn't hear any complaints last night when you held me."

"Last night I was . . ." a smirk curled on his lips, ". . . distracted."

Jessie pulled her lips into a thin line and shot him a look. "Don't start."

"Start what?" he said in his most innocent tone of voice. She opened her mouth to answer, but before she could say anything, he pulled her to standing. His arms went around her. He kissed her softly until he felt her surrender in his arms. "Is that what you didn't want to start?"

She took his face in her hands and held it gently. His breath softly fanned her face, his eyes caressed her. "I forget," she whispered. "You're pretty distracting yourself, you know."

He held her closer. "Do you regret letting me stay here on the couch?"

Jessie could see concern fill his eyes. Her gaze held his as she thought about the question. "No. But it might complicate things a little," she said softly. "Especially if someone saw your car in my driveway all night."

"I don't think anyone was out on patrol."

"Jarrett, you don't know Tempest."

"Then why did you let me stay?" he asked.

She managed a chuckle. "Because you looked like a lost puppy, and I'm a softie for sad eyes."

"That wasn't the reaction I had in mind," Jarrett confessed.

Jessie sighed. "Jarrett, everything is happening too fast. I'm afraid it'll get more complicated at work unless we slow down a little."

"I've wasted too much time already. Besides, it'll only get complicated if we let it. People are going to think what they want to think whether we like it or not. It's how we feel that's important."

She knew he was right, of course, but in a small town like Tempest, it didn't quite work that way.

"Speaking of work," she said, not willing to have to deal right now with thinking about the path that they had decided to take. "I do have to get to the hospital. Burrows is a stickler for promptness." He released her and she stepped out of his arms, looking at the magnificent breakfast he had prepared for her. "I wish you hadn't gone to so much trouble. I just don't eat much in the mornings."

"You used to," he said. He began to clear the table. "I guess I'll have to start taking notes on all the changes you've made over the years."

"Me too. You used to hate to cook."

"I still do. I was really just trying to impress you. But if it didn't work, I suppose I'll have to try something else."

Taking her hand, he pulled her to him. He closed his eyes and held his cheek to hers. "I won't ever hurt you again, Jess, I promise. This thing between us, it can work. Just give me the chance to prove it to you."

"I want to believe that, Jarrett," she answered in a voice that echoed her longings.

He stopped her with a kiss. "I know." He stroked her hair and nuzzled his nose against her cheek. "It's my fault you don't trust me. If you can't . . ."

Jessie felt him stiffen and pulled away to study his face. She searched anxiously for the meaning behind his words, but could only see apprehension in his eyes.

"I better get moving if I'm going to be on time," Jessie said. "Shouldn't you be starting rounds about now?"

Jarrett pretended not to notice the abrupt change of subject. "Not until ten."

Jessie said nothing more and hurried out of the room.

Jessie sat at her desk thinking about the man she left behind at her home. She was in trouble—a lot of it. The sooner the whole thing with him was resolved, the better for both of them. Despite all of her efforts, she was falling in love with him again. But there was no future together when he still seemed to refuse to open up to her completely.

"Miss O'Brien, the lady at billing said you could help me."

Startled back to reality by the voice, Jessie looked up from the pile of accounts on her desk. Dressed in a gray suit a shade darker than his thinning hair, a man of about sixty stood in front of her desk, shifting nervously from foot to foot. She smiled at him, not trusting her voice to be steady after mulling over her dilemma.

"You are Jessica O'Brien, the assistant comptroller, aren't you?" the man asked, his voice shaky.

"That I am. Please," she motioned to the empty chair in front of her desk, "sit down." She waited until he was settled. "What can I do for you?"

He cast his eyes down into his lap. "It's my wife." He looked back up. "She had a double bypass, but she's coming home today."

"That's wonderful. I'm glad she's better," Jessie replied, in a voice meant to reassure him.

The man twisted his hands together and continued to look into his lap. "She is, but there's a little problem."

Jessie put down the pen and straightened in her chair. "How can I help you?"

When the man finally looked back up, his eyes told her what he was going to say. She had seen that look a thousand times, and heard what followed it a thousand more. Just as she opened her mouth to reassure him that she understood his predicament, Gordon Burrows stormed into the room.

"Miss O'Brien, I need to see you in my office." His voice boomed as he strode by her with a fistful of papers in one hand and a crumpled computer printout in the other. He stopped at his office door and turned back to her. Only then did he notice that someone else was in the room. He looked at the man sitting across from her and nodded a polite greeting. "And bring the file you're working on with you when you're done here," he said, his voice more calm and even now.

The man waited until the echo of the door slamming died from the air before speaking. "Never mind; I see that you're busy here." He began to rise.

Jessie stood quickly and, reaching forward, put a hand to his arm to stop him from leaving. "No, sit. Please." She looked back toward Gordon's closed office door. "Don't let him scare you. He gets this way around the end of every month when it's time to balance the checkbook around here. His bark is much worse than his bite." She nodded at him. "Please, go on."

He sat back down and cleared his throat. "My wife is coming home today, and the nurse at the desk on the third floor suggested I check with billing so I could get an idea of how much the insurance would pay for." He dipped his head. "I thought the insurance was going to cover it all, but what will be left on the bill looks like it will come to about . . ." he pulled an invoice from the inside pocket of his suit jacket, ". . . $1200.00." He put it down on the desk. "Miss O'Brien, I don't have that kind of money. And if I tell my wife, she'll just get all upset again and end up right back where she was before the bypass."

Jessie spun the bill toward her and quickly scanned the charges. Most of his wife's stay in the cardiac care unit was paid for, but some of the more exotic cardiac tests were not covered by their medical insurance.

She looked back at him. "Mr., ah . . ." she glanced down at the hospital bill, ". . . Coleman, we can't have Mrs. Coleman . . ."

"Martha, her name is Martha."

Jessie smiled. "We can't let Martha get upset about anything. She has to use all her energy to concentrate on staying well so she doesn't have to come back here." She noticed he was relaxing, and she relaxed a bit herself. "I wish I could forgive this bill, but I can't."

"I'm not asking that," he said quickly. "For forty years, I've paid my way, mine and Martha's. I don't plan on stopping now." He reached for the wallet tucked in the rear pocket of his pants. "I can pay some, if that's okay, then I can pay a little every month." He pulled out two tens and put them on the desk. He looked at her, and then past her, toward the walnut grain of the door of the comptroller's office. "Is that enough for starters?"

Jessie reached into the right-hand desk drawer and removed one of the standard contracts. "I think we can work out something."

"But that man. Your boss." He nodded toward the oppressive wooden door behind her. "Don't you have to check with him?"

Jessie finished filling in the payment terms as she spoke, glancing up now and again to give him a reassuring smile. "Mr. Burrows, my boss, usually lets me handle this sort of thing." She looked up from the contract. "Now Mr. Coleman, what would be comfortable for you to pay us each month?"

Coleman fidgeted in the chair. "Let me see." He closed his eyes and began figuring. "Ten, fifty, a hundred and thirty, ninety-seven ... ah ... altogether about thirteen hundred. That leaves me with about a hundred or so left from the paycheck ..."

She stopped him right then. "Let's not forget incidentals, Mr. Coleman." She saw him bite down on his lip and realized he was misunderstanding her motives. "Let me help you," she said, filling in the contract amount. "Would fifteen dollars a month be too much for you?"

Mr. Coleman's eyes brightened and the worry line in his brow faded as a smile deepened the wrinkles around his mouth. "You mean it?"

Jessie stood and handed him the pen. "I sure do." After he signed the contract, she split the copies and handed the pink one to him. "When the obligation is finished, you'll get the top copy mailed to you stamped 'paid.' Is that all right, Mr. Coleman?"

He took the hand she extended in both of his own and shook it enthusiastically. "That would be great."

Jessie stuffed the remaining papers in a file that she would later mark with his name and final payment date. "You tell Mrs. Coleman I was asking about her."

"I sure will, Miss O'Brien. And just as soon as she feels up to it, I'm sure she'll bake you some of her famous homemade bread." He stood and walked into the hallway. "Thank you again," he said just before leaving.

Jessie leaned back in her chair. She felt good, real good. She clasped her hands over her stomach and smiled. The hospital would get its money and the Colemans wouldn't have to sell the family silver to do it. Sure Burrows would give her a rough time about the arrangements. He always did. But he'd just have to deal with the terms. She gathered up the file and began to rise when Jarrett appeared in the doorway.

"Hi. Miss me?" he asked with that devilishly handsome grin firmly set on his face as he leaned against the doorframe.

"Hi yourself," she replied, still organizing the folder.

"You haven't answered the question." He straightened and walked toward her.

She held out a hand to stop him. "Stay right where you are. Remember what almost happened last time you were here."

"Still worried about the rumor mill?" he asked, stopping at the other side of her desk.

"Not really."

"Good. Because we have a more immediate problem."

"We do?"

"Yep." He reached into his back pocket and pulled out a scrap of paper. "Here. Read this."

He leaned against the wall and crossed his arms over his chest while she read. The paper said:

There are six roses missing from my garden. If the thief will just come forward, nobody will get hurt. If not, I have to warn you all, Bruno will be on guard in the garden from now on.

The wife of the superintendent of Jessie's apartment complex had signed it.

Jessie grimaced. "Does she know it was you raiding her roses?"

He took the paper from her and tucked it back into his pocket. "No. This was stuck in everyone's door this morning. She must have done it sometime after you left for work."

Jessie tilted her head. "You know, it's my duty to see that justice prevails here."

Jarrett dropped his hands and let his shoulders fall. "You're right. I can't run forever."

"It's better this way. Believe me, you can't run from Bruno anyway."

"Big dog, huh?"

Jessie shook her head. "No, nasty cat." She curled her fingers. "He has the sharpest claws I ever felt. I remember one time I was passing by and reached down to pet him. I was just trying to be friendly, but Bruno thought otherwise." She angled the back of her hand to him. "I have the scars to prove it."

"So you're saying that unless I come clean with the landlady, Bruno's going to hurt me."

"Seems so."

"And you could be viewed as my accomplice. The evidence is in your kitchen." He held up his hands, wrists pressed together. "Then do your duty and take me in. Looks like my career is in your hands."

A secretive smile softened her lips. She moved around to the front of the desk and leaned against it. "Why Dr. Collins, surrendering to protect my reputation. How heroic of you."

"Chivalry is alive and well in Tempest," Jarrett said with a laugh.

Jessie laughed with him. "Well, Sir Jarrett, I hope you parked your white horse in the reserved area at least."

Their laughter brought Gordon Burrows out from his office. He glared back and forth from Jessie to Jarrett. "Miss O'Brien, I believe we had a date." He colored fiercely with the misstatement. "What I mean is that when I come back from bookkeeping, I'd like to start our meeting." He walked into the hallway.

"I'll be ready," she called out as he disappeared into the corridor.

Jarrett gave her a puzzled look. "Did I walk in on something important?"

Jessie turned the upper part of her body to the left to scoop up the rest of the papers on her desk. "Depends on your perspective." She held up the file. "Gordon walked in on another one of my payment-arranging sessions, and I think I'm about to get read the riot act."

"Is there anything I can do?"

"No." Her hand moved absently to her hair, a sign she was already building her attack plan in her mind. "Just get out of here and let me do my job while I still have one."

He leaned over and kissed her lightly. "Will I see you later?"

"I don't know." She straightened. "I have that fund-raiser dinner tonight and you have a date with a sweet little cherub up on three."

Disregarding the fact they were still in her office, he pulled her into his arms and, in deference to her sense of privacy, pushed the door to her office shut with his foot so no one would see them from the hallway.

His eyes roamed over her face. "Afterward, suppose I come by and try to tempt another sweet angel into falling from grace?"

"I'd say you can try, but don't be so sure of the outcome," she answered.

Seated at his large mahogany desk, Gordon Burrows looked over the top of his reading glasses at Jessie and glared. "How in the world do you expect me to convince the Board of Trustees that you're the right person for my job when you keep doing this?" As he shook the Coleman file in the air, a few pieces of paper fluttered onto the desk. Jessie reached out to gather them, but Burrows waved her off. "This hospital is just barely making a profit and we have the expansion project to fit into next year's budget somehow."

Jessie braced herself for the usual lecture about debits and credits, profits and losses, and let him run through it completely before speaking up. "Gordon, we've had this conversation a hundred times already. I can't, in good conscience, take a man's last dime to satisfy his bill when I know it will hurt him and his family in the long run." She stood, walked to the credenza, and poured herself a cup of six-hour-old coffee just to work off some of her restless energy. "Besides, I've checked. Just for the record, not once has anyone defaulted on the payment schedule I've arranged."

"Yes, but once the patient died before the contract was satisfied."

Jessie spun around to face him. "Gordon, that's cold." She gulped down the nasty brew and returned to the chair. "But that's not what this meeting is really about, is it?"

"What do you mean?" He opened the side drawer and pulled out a peppermint. "Want one?" he asked, unwrapping the cellophane.

Jessie declined. "Come on, Gordon, you're stalling. You always eat when you're nervous, so I know you didn't call me in here to yell about another payment contract. You know that I'm not about to change the way I do my job. I've been doing it the same way for the past five years."

"And I've been letting you get away with it."

"I think we've established that a long time ago, so

don't tap dance around the real issue." She walked back to the chair and sat down. "Out with it."

Gordon moved some papers around on his desk before speaking. "Jessie, you know I've been grooming you for years to take over for me when I retire in a few months."

"And I appreciate that very much."

Folding his hands on the desktop, Gordon slowly leaned forward. "We may have a problem."

"About my work?"

Gordon shook his head. "There's no easy way to say this."

"Then get it over with."

Gordon hesitated, then went on. "Pritch Stewart cornered me near the coffee shop this morning and conned me into buying her some decaf. I had to spend the first half hour of my day with her."

"I guess that explains why you're so grumpy," Jessie said with a nervous laugh.

Gordon was not amused. "A little respect, Jessie. Pritch is one of the cornerstones of this community, and her husband is on the Board of Trustees of this hospital."

"And she's the town busybody."

"That very well may be, but she's very influential and very driven."

"I'm well aware of that. The Stewart Cardiac Pavilion is a part of the expansion plan, isn't it?"

"Yes."

"I suppose Pritch went into her tirade about making sure that 'her' wing stays in next year's capital improvement program no matter what else has to go."

Gordon's face sobered. "Not this time, Jessie."

His serious tone began to concern Jessie. "If not the dollars and cents to pay for the plaque with her name on it for the cornerstone, then what did she want with you?"

Burrows shifted slightly in his chair. "She wanted to talk about you." He looked away. "You and Dr. Collins."

Jessie tried to read his eyes, but they had gone steely. Taken by surprise by the shift to her relationship with Jarrett, she hesitated. Pritch could be a problem. Besides being one of the wealthiest contributors to the hospital, she wore the pants in the Stewart family. "What was it that she wanted to know?"

Appearing uncharacteristically nervous, Gordon began to play with his pen as he spoke. "She had some questions about your relationship with Dr. Collins." He saw her stiffen and reacted to it. "But I told her I didn't know a thing, and that the personal life of hospital employees was really not any of my concern as long as it did not affect job performance, and that your performance on the job was exemplary."

"Thank you, Gordon," Jessie said. "Did that satisfy her?"

"Not exactly. She said she's been hearing things; things that are causing her concern."

"What kind of things?" Jessie took a breath to temper her anger. Her personal life was none of Pritch Stewart's business.

"You said Dr. Collins told you why he came to Midwest Medical, didn't you?"

"Sort of."

"Then he told you about his messy divorce. Apparently it was quite scandalous."

Jessie opened her mouth to speak but the shock of what Gordon had just told her choked off the words. She hoped her face wasn't betraying her ignorance. She thought about last night with Jarrett. Although they did discuss some things, the evening hadn't lent itself to too much talking toward the end, unless you happen to count sweet-talking.

"Hedidntgettothatpartexactly," she mumbled.

Gordon's brows lowered. "I didn't quite catch all of that."

"He didn't get to that part." A dull ache began at her temples. "But I'm sure he meant to tell me."

"Good intentions aside," Gordon said quite seriously, "I think you need to know that Pritch is just about convinced that he was driven out of New York General and didn't leave voluntarily."

"And how did she come to that conclusion?"

"She said she made a few calls back to the hospital and although no one would confirm her suspicion, no one would deny it either."

In the span of one split second, Jessie had to decide if she finally had part of the answer to the question that had been nagging her almost since Jarrett had come back into her life. His leaving New York couldn't have been part of just turning tail and running. If it were, he would have told her, wouldn't he? He couldn't have held her in his arms and kissed her the way he had if it was all merely part of an escape. Maybe what Pritch heard was merely the rumor mill grinding out dirt about the new doctor in town.

Now she had another decision to make. Head or heart.

It suddenly was an easy choice. She went with her heart. "I don't believe that, Gordon. Not for one minute."

Gordon's face was sullen. "There's more, Jessie. Pritch suggested that the only reason he's cozying up to you is so you'll use your influence to help him get entrenched in his position here."

That stopped her for a moment. She kept her voice deceptively calm in the face of her growing anxiety. "Gordon, that doesn't make any sense. You know I have nothing to do with hiring practices or placements."

"But you do work with most of the hospital's hierarchy."

Jessie held up her hands in a defensive pose. "Gordon, are you telling me that Pritch Stewart thinks I would use some type of leverage to get Dr. Collins some type of tenure?" She vaulted out of her chair, a vein pulsing angrily at her throat. "Cozy up to the Board to get him some type of . . . of what?"

"Now calm down, Jessie. I told Pritch that she was being ridiculous about the whole matter. I told her you were the most honest person I know and that I would trust you with everything I owned."

"And?"

"She backed off a little. But you know this place. Once a story's been started, it doesn't matter what the truth is. The only thing people remember is what they choose to believe." He leaned back. "I'm sorry to have to tell you this, but I think she's trying to talk her husband into asking the Board to convene an ethics hearing on the matter."

Shock and anger rippled up Jessie's spine. "This is insane, Gordon. Are you telling me that Jarrett's career and my job are on the line now?"

"I don't know."

Jessie flashed him a look of disdain. "I think you do. I think you're telling me that if I continue to see Dr. Collins before the Board of Trustees makes their decision on your replacement, I may be sitting on the other side of that door for quite a while." She jerked her right thumb over her shoulder.

Gordon held up his hands in a don't-shoot pose. "Jessie, I honestly don't know. I just thought you should know the situation I'm up against here."

"And what about Jarrett? You know as well as I do that an ethics hearing could turn into a witch hunt if Pritch thinks Jarrett's position here would have the slightest effect on the fund-raising efforts for her precious hospital wing."

Gordon watched her closely as she moved around his office. "You know as well as I do that if Pritch wants an inquiry, she'll get one."

Jessie rose, and, arms folded across her chest, began to pace. "That's ridiculous. He's a wonderful doctor, capable, caring, and competent. If the Board thought there was going to be a problem of any type, then he should have never been put on staff."

Gordon's voice took on an apologetic tone. "A small town like Tempest is apt to do things a little backwards sometimes. We're just going to have to be patient and see what develops."

Jessie gritted her teeth. "See what develops? I'll tell you what I hope develops, Gordon. For what she's about to do, I hope that Pritch Stewart catches a rip-roaring case of lockjaw, and that Dr. Jarrett Collins is the only one with the cure."

Chapter Nine

J essie had to talk to Jarrett before she went to the fund-raiser dinner. He had no idea what gossip could do to someone in a small town like Tempest. Reputation was a fragile thing, something easily and eternally destroyed.

As she dressed, she could hardly concentrate on what to wear, but decided on a stylish lavender silk shirt and a long skirt of the same color. The sash pulling it all together was a muted pastel print of wildflowers. She looked at herself in the full-length bedroom mirror and was grateful she didn't look as unstrung as she felt.

She was bothered by the stares she'd endured at work: in the hallways, in the coffee shop, even walking through the parking lot. No one considered her that interesting before Jarrett came to Tempest. But now that she was dating him there was some dirt in the air.

She quickly scolded herself. She shouldn't begin

thinking like the rest of them. But with all the rumors swirling around, she was finding it difficult to think about anything else. She felt unsure about a lot of things, but especially about how she was going to be able to carry off the evening if she didn't set some questions to rest.

She thought about the day at the batting cages, and remembered how he warned her that everything they did in life came with a price. She scooped up her beaded purse from the bed and took a deep breath. It was time to find out just how much a life with Jarrett was going to cost.

Jessie's heels echoed down the nearly empty hospital hallway as she made her way to the elevators. A few people either nodded in her direction or gave her a quick wave as they headed home for the weekend or came on duty.

She glanced at her watch. It was six. With the cocktail party beginning at seven and dinner at eight, she had time to find Jarrett and still make it in time for the welcoming speech. There would be no time for heavy discussion about anything, however. That would come later. Right now he needed to know what was being said. And she needed to know if it was true.

She was sinking fast. What she felt when Gordon told her what Pritch wanted to do to Jarrett was beyond anything she had felt before. It was like someone had reached into her chest and squeezed her heart. Her first instinct was to circle the wagons around him and protect. Her second was to prove that Pritch was wrong.

As she thought about it now, it wasn't either of those emotions that made her sit up and take notice. If she closed her eyes she could feel it pulsating deep within her soul. There was no question any longer. She still loved him. And she had to tell him. In a short span of time and maybe even against her better judgement, she had let him become as much a part of her life now as he had been so many years earlier. She swallowed back the feeling of uneasiness that hit her at the same time the realization did; as careful as she had been, he was back in her heart as though he had never left it.

The elevator doors opened to the third floor. She heard muted voices and two distinct sets of footsteps heading away from her. One set was slow with long strides, landing clearly and crisply on the vinyl floor. The other set shuffled with small steps, sounding like the gentle patting of ballet shoes sliding across the floor.

Jessie stepped out from the elevator car and looked in the direction of the sounds. Sandy and Jarrett were in the distance.

Sandy wore a pink robe and matching slippers. Her dark hair fell softly down her back. In one hand, she gripped the teddy bear Jessie had given her by its ear, its feet skimming the floor as she shuffled along. Her other hand was tucked inside Jarrett's.

Jessie felt like an intruder in a scene from a Norman Rockwell painting. The good doctor, white coat, stethoscope around his neck, walking with his small charge, apparently talking about things only important to them. When they disappeared into the room, Jessie followed, but stayed in the hall, careful not to make a sound.

She stood silent and watched. At the foot of the hospital bed Sandy let go of Jarrett's hand. She put the teddy bear under the covers and raised her arms to him. "I need some help. That's awful high for me to get in by myself. 'Specially with my leg not working so good anymore."

Jarrett smiled and scooped her into his arms. He sat her on the edge of the bed and removed her slippers, letting them drop with a soft thud to the floor. Sandy scooted herself backward, giggling as she pulled the covers up and tucked them around her waist.

"Now," she said, placing the teddy bear in the crook of her arm, "if you could raise the head part, I'll sit up and talk to you until my mommy comes up from talking to the therapy guy."

Dutifully Jarrett moved to the foot of the bed and pulled out the hand crank. "Tell me when," he said, turning the handle in big looping circles and watching the top of the bed rise.

"When," Sandy said when she was satisfied with the angle. She patted the mattress. "You sit here while we talk, okay?"

"Sure." Jarrett sat on the edge of the bed. He reached out and brushed her bangs away from the bandage on her forehead. "How does your head feel now that the stitches are out?"

Sandy fingered the gauze over her wound. "Good. I was feeling all itchy before. Mommy said it was because I was getting better."

"Your mom was right."

Sandy dropped her hand and dipped her head. "Could I ask you something really important, Dr. Jarrett?"

"Ask away."

"And you'll tell me for true?"

He nodded.

"Cross your heart?"

He made the sign with his right hand. "Cross my heart."

Sandy's face became serious. She moved the bear out of the way and sat up straight. "Will I always walk crooked like that? I mean, my right leg isn't working the way it used to before I cracked my head open. I kinda have to pull it now."

Jarrett leaned closer to her. "You know Sandy, that's really up to you and how hard you work with . . ." he tapped the tip of her nose with his forefinger. ". . . The therapy guy."

"Why?"

"You hit your head pretty hard that day." He reached out and lightly touched her forehead.

"Yeah I know." She furrowed her brows thoughtfully. "Hey, did some of my brains fall out before you sewed up the hole? Is that why I walk funny?"

Jarrett's mouth lifted in a smile. "Not exactly." He took her hand. The skin was a dark purple-blue in the area where the paramedics had inserted the IV needle at the accident site. "See this bruise?" He drew a circle around the discoloration with the tip of his finger.

"Yep."

"Well, your brain has a bruise like this on it from when you hit your head. It needs time to heal itself before it can begin to send the right messages to your leg."

Sandy poked at the bruise with her fingers. "Does the one inside my head look as yucky?"

Jarrett nodded. "I imagine it does. But just like this one, it's getting better every day." It wasn't quite that simple, but the analogy was the only one he could think of that Sandy might understand.

Sandy looked back up at him. "So how long is it gonna take for my brain to tell my leg to work right?"

"I don't know for sure. That's why you have to keep going to therapy. The exercises you do there will help remind your brain what it's supposed to tell your leg to do when you want to walk, and you'll get better a lot faster."

Sandy crossed her hands over her chest and hunkered down in the bed. "I don't like the therapy guy too much. He's not as nice as you are. He makes me walk and walk and walk." She pushed out her lower lip and inclined her head. "Why can't you be my therapy guy?"

Jarrett shook his head. "I can't do that, honey. Your therapy guy can do a much better job for you than I can because he went to school and studied hard so he could help you get better."

To Sandy, the solution was simple. "So stop being a doctor and go to the same school the therapy guy did."

"I can't do that either."

"Why?"

"Because I like what I do."

Sandy reached over and played with the end of Jarrett's stethoscope. "Did you always want to be a doctor?"

He nodded. "Always."

"And did you always want to take care of kids?"

"Yes, and grownups too."

"How about dogs?"

Jarrett laughed. "Then I'd be a vet. That's an animal doctor."

Sandy reached for the teddy bear. "I know that. I was just asking." She tucked the bear under the covers. "What would you do if you couldn't be a doctor?"

Jarrett sighed. "I don't know. I don't think I could be anything else."

"You could come live with us," Sandy said enthusiastically.

He laughed again. "You better check with your mom and dad first."

"I will." Her eyes began to flutter as she fought off the coming sleep. "Could I ask you just one more thing?"

Jarrett slid from the bed and began to crank it back down. "Ask away."

"Do you have any kids I can play with once my leg gets better?"

The question caused a lump to rise in Jarrett's throat. He swallowed it back. "No. But I always wanted some."

Nearly asleep, Sandy didn't notice the past tense. "How come?"

He pulled the covers up and tucked them around her chin. "Because," he said, his voice wavering just enough to be noticeable. "I don't have someone to marry yet."

Sandy yawned and shifted to one side. "Why doesn't anyone like you enough to marry you?"

"Maybe someone will someday." Jarrett stroked Sandy's hair with one hand as he spoke. Her angel face, eyes closed in near-sleep, brought back memories of the many nights he would daydream about having a family of his own.

"Maybe you can marry that lady who brought me in the ambulance," Sandy said innocently.

"Oh, I don't think so right now."

"Why not? She's nice." Sandy rubbed her eyes and covered her mouth as she yawned.

"We used to know each other a long time ago, but we haven't talked to each other for a while."

"Did you have a fight or something?"

Jarrett laughed. "Sort of."

Sandy tapped her small forefinger on her chin. "I

know. I'll tell her that you're sorry and that she shouldn't be mad at you anymore."

"I don't think she's mad at me anymore," Jarrett said.

"Good. Then you can get married with her." Sandy yawned again and let her head fall to one side. In moments she was asleep.

Jarrett sat silent, watching the rise and fall of Sandy's chest in peaceful sleep. Her cherub mouth was pursed in a slight smile and her long lashes shaded her cheeks. He smiled at the simplicity of her solution. If only it could be that easy.

"I should have married her a long time ago," he whispered right before he leaned over and kissed Sandy on the cheek.

As he looked at Sandy, he realized that the only time he seemed to be at peace anymore was when he was with Jessie. He wondered why and answered the question almost immediately. He needed her. Always had. Even as he ran from her because he loved her too much, he needed her. He only allowed himself to finally admit it when his life plummeted out of control without her and he was helpless to stop it. It was only since he'd found her again that he felt he was really going to be all right. He was risking everything by not telling her the whole truth about his marriage. He had to tell her the rest before someone else did. But after he did, would she be able to forgive him for waiting so long?

Back inside the elevator, Jessie closed her eyes and leaned her head against the cold metal walls, not knowing what to do. She felt the prickle of tears beneath her eyelids.

All too clearly she had heard the quaver in Jarrett's

voice when he spoke to Sandy, saw his hand shake when he reached out to stroke her hair as she slept. She could almost feel his pain. It was obvious he was hurting very badly and didn't want her to know how much.

She wanted to run to him, hold him, and tell him she wanted to help. But how could she if he wouldn't tell her what he needed her to do? Were the rumors true? When he came to Tempest, was he merely running from his past? Or was he running *to* it, as he had said?

Jarrett sat on the well-worn green vinyl couch in the doctors' lounge, elbows resting on his knees, aching head in his hands. He needed some time alone to gather his scattered emotions and file them back away.

He leaned his head against the back of the couch, spread his arms across the top of the cushions, and closed his eyes. Make it go away, he pleaded silently. Just make the last ten years ago away and let me start over with Jessie. He heard the door open. Without moving, he raised his eyelids only far enough to see who was coming into the lounge. It was Steve Silberberg, the head of the department. And he didn't look at all happy.

"Collins, I've been looking for you." Steve was dressed in a T-shirt, jeans, and a pair of sneakers that had seen better days; atypical dress for the Head of Staff.

"I've been here," Jarrett said.

"You look like heck."

Jarrett looked at his watch. It was nine already. Had he really been sitting in the doctors' lounge for over two hours? He straightened and ran a hand through his hair. "What brings you out this time of night? I thought you and Nina were closing up the house at the lake." He leaned forward and rested his forearms on his thighs before looking up at Steve.

"I've been there and back." Steve slid one of the tattered chairs away from the wall and placed it directly across from Jarrett. "There's a problem."

Uncomfortable with the tone of Silberberg's voice, Jarrett sat up straight. "Must be a big one to bring you back here."

Steve sat. He crossed his arms in front of his chest. "It could be."

Jarrett heard a warning siren go off inside his head. "You're being a bit cryptic, Steve."

"I don't know how to tell you this."

"Straightforward is usually the best way."

Silberberg hesitated for a moment before speaking. "Jarrett, I got a call from Simonson about ten minutes after I got to the lake."

"Herb Simonson? The head of the Ethics Committee? What did he want with you on a Friday night after-hours?"

Steve grabbed the sides of his chair and hauled his frame up to a full sitting position. "He's convening a hearing on Monday morning," he said with deceptive calm. Jarrett gave him a perfunctory nod. "Look, Jarrett, you're a good doctor and there's no easy way to say this, so here goes. A few of the trustees have been hearing things, things they want to clear up, and . . ."

Jarrett cut him off. "Wait a minute. Do you mean the Ethics Committee is convening a hearing on me?"

Steve nodded.

A stab of feelings, like a message across the darkness, telegraphed themselves into Jarrett's mind. He set them aside for the moment. "You said the committee's been hearing things. What kind of things?" he asked, searching anxiously for the meaning behind Silberberg's words.

"There's been some talk about what happened back in New York and . . ."

"You mean about my divorce?"

"I'm sorry."

Jarrett bolted to his feet. "This is ridiculous. My personal life has nothing to do with my medical skill." He ran an angry hand through his hair and walked to the window. He spun back around. "We talked a little about it during the interview. Any questions should have been asked then."

Steve walked over to him and put a hand on his shoulder. "I recommended putting you on staff. I'm not the one who needs any convincing about your skill and commitment to medicine."

Jarrett stared at him. "Can they do this?" he asked anxiously.

"This isn't the big city, Collins. Tempest is a small town with a big, expensive hospital. And Pritch Stewart is this hospital's biggest benefactor. I don't have to tell you what that means, do I?"

Jarrett shook his head.

"Listen, take the rest of the night off. You're not scheduled in this weekend, are you?"

"No. But I had some plans."

"I think your plans have just changed. Use the weekend to get ready." Steve stuck out his hand. "If it's any consolation, I think you're a heck of a doctor, Collins. I'd hate to lose you."

Jarrett looked down at the hand extended to him and grasped it firmly. "Thanks."

For a long time after Steve left, Jarrett stood looking out of the second-floor lounge window. It appeared as though fate had dealt its hand, and he had no recourse but to play along.

Jessie felt like a nervous cat. Would this party ever be over? If she looked at her watch once, she looked at it a hundred times, and each time only a minute or so had passed. It was nearly ten P.M. Dinner was over, the speeches had ended, and in about another hour, she'd be ushering the last of the stragglers to the door and out to the parking lot.

Jessie didn't hear Ann approaching until she was right next to her. "Great party, Jess."

Ann's voice made Jessie nearly jump out of her skin. "A little warning next time would be nice," Jessie said, taking a deep breath to calm her racing pulse. "I see you decided on the blue dress. You look great in it."

"Thanks. By the way, exactly where were you a moment ago? It's obvious you weren't here."

"Very funny. I guess I'm a little distracted, that's all."

"By a handsome doctor, I'll bet." Ann leaned closer. She grinned impishly. "I gotta know, he's got such a great-looking mouth. Is he a good kisser?"

Jessie arched an eyebrow at her friend. "Ann, I can't believe you would ask me something like that."

"Better me asking than Peggy."

"Is she here too?"

Anne gestured to the front of the room. "She's at Pritch's table."

Jessie groaned and looked over. Pritch and Peggy had their heads together, undoubtedly filling each other in on last-minute gossip. "Look at them. I'll just bet they're tearing him up."

"You two have been the hot topic of conversation lately," Ann volunteered.

"I guessed as much." Jessie scanned the room. A few people were looking in her direction. She knew she should just ignore them, but she couldn't. She didn't like being the subject of speculation and rumor.

Ann's tone became serious. "I have to warn you, people aren't going to stop talking until they satisfy their curiosity. And, you know as well as I do, that what they don't know, they'll make up to fill in the blanks."

Jessie had no response. She knew Ann was right.

Jarrett adjusted the tie at the neck of his tuxedo shirt and grabbed the jacket from the back of the chair. He glanced at the clock on top of the entertainment center and walked to the door. He had just enough time to get to the hall at McKay's and find Jessie in time for the last dance.

At the door he closed his eyes and practiced what he was going to say to her. "I love you, Jessie. I've loved you since the day we were in your aunt's wedding. I've made a lot of mistakes since then, but if you'll let me, I'll spend the rest of my life making every one of them up to you." He had never stopped loving Jessie. He knew that now. The years had proved it to him. All he had to do now was convince Jessie.

If she would let him do that, and if she would let him love her enough, then the secrets he would tell her wouldn't matter.

Would they?

Jessie looked toward the door and saw Matt and his wife coming toward her. Quickly she put on a smile.

"Another success," she said, trying to distract herself from what she was really thinking about.

"Seems so. Have some champagne." Matt plucked a tall fluted glass from the tray of a passing waiter and handed it to her. "You deserve to celebrate. To a new ambulance," he said, raising his glass in a toast. "I can almost see the purchase order now."

Although celebrating was the farthest thing from Jessie's mind, she touched her glass to Matt and Carrie's before taking a small sip. "You deserve most of the credit."

Matt finished his champagne and put the empty glass on the table behind him. "Actually, Carrie does." He looped his arm around his wife's waist. "This black-tie affair was her idea. I didn't think we'd get three people to spend two hundred dollars a ticket, but Carrie said all we had to do was get the word around." He leaned over and kissed her on the cheek. "And she was right."

Carrie blushed. "It really wasn't all that hard. You know what happens in Tempest once people start talking."

Jessie felt her stomach lurch. "What do you mean?" Grateful her voice hadn't quavered, she took a longer sip of the champagne to calm herself.

Carrie lowered her voice. "All I did was tell Pritch Stewart that the Andersons were buying a whole table of ten. Then, not to be outdone, Pritch bought two tables. Then the Conways heard about what Pritch did and bought a table, then the Andersons really did buy ten tickets, fortunately for me, and it just spiraled out from there."

Matt gave his wife an affectionate squeeze. "That's my girl, using that rumor mill for good for a change."

Jessie gulped down the rest of her drink and felt it

begin to go to her head. "However you got it done, Carrie, it's wonderful." She hiccuped and raised her fingers to her lips. "Sorry. Champagne always does that to me." In the background, the five-piece band began to play again.

Matt took the empty glasses from his wife's hand. "Jess, I'd ask you to dance, but my dance card's all filled up." He spun Carrie into his arms and nibbled on her ear. "Later, lady, you and I are going to work on that daughter you've been wanting."

Carrie feigned shock. "Matt, you devil." She turned her head to Jessie as Matt began to dance her away. "He gets like this when he has too much champagne." She winked. "But I like it."

Jessie hoped her smile wasn't as sad as it felt when she watched them glide away from her. As she watched, she saw Matt whisper something into Carrie's ear. Carrie threw back her head in laughter. Matt countered by spinning Carrie in his arms and dipping her low before raising her back up slowly and kissing her neck, much to her delight and to that of those around them on the dance floor. Matt and Carrie never seemed so happy.

And Jessie had never felt so alone.

Chapter Ten

The dinner-dance was finally drawing to a close. People were filtering out the door. Jessie was leaning across a table to pick up an empty wineglass and a crumpled mauve linen napkin when she saw Jarrett.

"I thought I'd surprise you."

His voice flowed over her, warming the cold hollows of her worried nerves. Slowly she straightened, letting her gaze run up the length of his frame as she did. His tuxedo fit perfectly. The dark vest led to the pure white of his tuxedo shirt, with the black bow tie at his neck splitting the formality of his dress from the buoyancy of his smile. His smile lit his eyes, making her suddenly forget everything but him.

"What are you doing here?" she managed to say, putting the glass and the napkin down.

He stepped around the table. "I couldn't wait until tomorrow to see you. I hope you don't mind." She started to respond, when a most unladylike hiccup greeted him. He laughed and swept her into his arms. "You've been drinking champagne without me."

Her body bounced with another hiccup. "Just let me hold my breath for a few minutes and they'll be gone," she promised, inhaling.

"Here, let me help you," Jarrett volunteered right before he confined her mouth in a kiss.

As he tenderly kissed her, Jessie's body would not let her breathe, and the hiccups vanished. Jarrett's cure had worked perfectly.

In the background, the band began to play a slow number. A few of the remaining couples drifted out onto the dance floor. "Let's dance," Jarrett said, smiling against her lips. "I like holding you." His eyes never left hers as they walked onto the dance floor together.

Jessie placed one hand on his shoulder, while the other remained cradled in his. He said nothing more, but whirled her to the center of the floor. Overhead the multi-colored ball turned, spilling a thousand tinted lights across them. Never taking their eyes from each other, they moved as one to the slow beat of the song that wrapped around them. In Jarrett's eyes a gamut of feelings dimmed and brightened, each one telling Jessie without words that this thing between them was destined to be.

And it made her tremble because she knew he was right.

He took his hand from her waist and touched her hair. "Jessie," he whispered, "you give me so much when I'm with you." He moved his lips to her cheek. "Tell me you feel the same way." His words were lost to her as their lips touched once more. They moved in unison to the soft music that surrounded them, his kisses sweet, understanding, coaxing a response from her.

When the music stopped and they parted, he brought his hands to her face and cupped her cheeks. He looked deep into her eyes. "I love you, Jessie. I need you in my life. You give me the peace I thought I would never have."

The urgency in his voice frightened her. "Jarrett, I don't know what to say to you."

"Say you love me, Jessie. Even if you don't mean it, I need to hear you say it." Another number began, but he ignored it. He pulled her into another kiss. When he moved his kiss to her temple, his voice rumbled past her ear. "You do love me, don't you, Jessie?"

She pulled away from him to catch her breath. Over his shoulder she could see that everyone around them had stopped dancing and had turned to watch. Heads were bent low in whispered conversation, and a few couples were openly staring. Her gaze darted back and forth between Jarrett and the people surrounding them.

Jarrett picked up on Jessie's body language and stepped away from her. "I suppose we are a little conspicuous here. Is there some other place we can talk?"

Jessie looked over her shoulder and motioned toward a set of French doors leading to a small terrace. "Out there?"

He nodded. "I'll be out in a minute," he said.

She smiled and pressed her palm to his cheek. He cupped her hand with his and turned his face to kiss its softness. As she walked to the terrace, her heart was aching in anticipation of what he would say to her. Throwing open the doors, she wondered why the wonderful declaration of love she had just heard from Jarrett could make her feel such despair.

* * *

Outside, she sat on one of the white wicker chairs surrounding a matching small table. Through the pane of glass to her left she could see the band packing its equipment in the far corner of the room, and noticed the remaining guests gathering their belongings to leave.

She looked out into the night, toward the lights of the small town. Jarrett's actions, although wonderfully romantic, had been very cryptic. She knew there could only be one reason for his acting the way he had: he knew about the committee hearing. She wondered if she should come right out and let him know that she knew about it too, but quickly decided against that tack. If he felt this urgency to find her and tell her of the situation himself, then she should let him. Building a new sense of trust between them was something she knew they would have to go through together.

She heard the handle on the doors turn, and watched in silence as Jarrett joined her.

"Here," he said, walking onto the brick terrace with two fluted glasses in his hands.

"Aren't you afraid I'll spend the evening hiccuping? Although I have to admit, I do like the cure, Doctor." Jessie rose from the chair and walked toward him. "Are we celebrating something?"

He smiled. "No, we're remembering something."

When she got closer, she noticed that the glasses were filled with a dark brown liquid. She took one from him, a spark of excitement rippling through her. She raised the goblet to her lips, a smile overtaking them as she tasted. "Cola." A rush of tenderness overwhelmed her.

He nodded. "Do you remember the last time we drank cola from champagne glasses?"

"How could I forget? It was at my aunt's wedding."

She looked down at the shiny, leather shoes on his feet. "But you were wearing white high-top sneakers with your tuxedo then."

He laughed. Putting a hand to the small of her back, he eased her to the chair. "We danced all night."

"You hadn't wanted to dance at all at first," she amended, sitting and putting down her glass. "You wouldn't even hold my hand."

"Fortunately, I got over that," he added, setting his glass next to hers on the table.

"No one could get you to sit still once you finally got moving." A tinkle of laughter escaped from Jessie's throat. "I think you danced with every female in the place."

Jarrett chuckled. "But you were the only one who got cola in a champagne glass."

"I remember feeling so special when you did that." Her memories of that day were still fresh and clear. "On the way back to Wisconsin on the plane, I told my grandmother that I was going to marry you and . . ."

In one fluid motion, Jarrett pulled her to her feet and into his arms. "It should have been you."

His lips came down on hers in a kiss full of love and need, making the blood pound in her brain and the beat leap from her heart. She never wanted it to end.

Jarrett pulled away with reluctance. He stroked her hair and ran his knuckles down her cheek. "Jessie, there's something else you need to know before I can let this go any further." He stepped away from her and walked to the edge of the terrace. He shoved his hands deep into the pockets of his tuxedo pants and sighed.

Jessie was beside him in an instant. "Whatever it is, Jarrett, just tell me," she said in a voice that was no more than a whisper.

Surprised, he turned to her. "It isn't pretty, Jessie. I want you to know up front that I'll understand if you want to just wash your hands of me right here and now after I tell you."

She put a hand to his shoulder and he reached up with his to hold it fast. "Tell me, Jarrett."

They walked back to the chairs and Jessie sat down. Jarrett stood, unable to contain his restless energy. He unhooked the bow tie at his neck and folded it into his inside coat pocket. He released the top three buttons of his tuxedo shirt as he spoke. "You don't know everything about me."

A creeping uneasiness at the bottom of her heart began to spread upward, cooling the crackling fire in her stomach and replacing it with cold lucidity. "I knew you very well before you went off to medical school." She exchanged glances with him before adding, "I'm sure a lot of that person is still in there somewhere." She reached out and touched his chest. "I've seen him a lot over the past few weeks."

"I sure hope so." His voice was low and sad.

Jessie swallowed back the unpleasantness that welled up from her stomach. "Go on."

Jarrett pinched the bridge of his nose and ran his fingers across his eyes. "When I left you for medical school, I had no intentions of getting involved with anyone else."

"But you did. You told me this already, Jarrett. You got married."

Jarrett raised his hands in a defensive pose. "It wasn't quite that simple. In fact, it's very complicated."

"I think I'm about to find that out," Jessie said in a shaky voice.

Jarrett raked his hair back with his fingers and began to pace. "Angie . . ."

"Your wife."

"My ex-wife," he corrected, "was the daughter of the head of the medical school. Some guy or another seemed to be always trying to get to her. Somehow we developed a friendship because she knew it was all I wanted from her. I didn't want to replace you." Jessie lowered her gaze to the ground with the words. Taking her hand, Jarrett fell to one knee beside her to look into her eyes. "We got close over the next few months. I became kind of like her protector. Then things began to happen so fast."

"What kind of things?"

The look on Jessie's face was enough to make him panic. "It's not what you're thinking."

"Are you asking me or telling me what to think?" Jessie muttered as her anger began to rise. How dare he presume she would just sit here and let him tell her about his courtship of his ex-wife.

"I never meant for anything serious to happen, but somehow she convinced me that we were meant to be together."

"So you married her."

"You make it sound so . . ."

"Simple," Jessie finished for him. She pulled back her hand and rose. She walked to the French doors and folded her arms in front of her. "So you played Prince Charming and married the princess."

He rose and walked to her. "Have a little mercy and let me explain." Placing both hands on her shoulders, he turned her to face him. "You feel like ice, Jessie." He peeled off his jacket. "Here, take this," he said, draping it over her shoulders.

"Thanks." She grabbed the lapels and pulled the

jacket tightly around her. She was cold, but she wasn't sure whether it was from the night air or from what she had just heard.

He rubbed his hands up and down her arms to help warm her as he spoke. "The whole thing took only about three months."

The tensing of her jaw betrayed her frustrations. "A whirlwind romance." She took a few steps away from him. "Is that what you came here to tell me?"

"No. Yes. Some. But that was the easy part."

Intrigued, Jessie walked back to the wicker chair and sat down. She could find no words to describe how she felt at this moment.

Jarrett continued. "It didn't take long before I realized the mistake I had made. It was like Angie transformed. What came out was someone I never knew could exist." The line of Jarrett's mouth tightened a fraction more, and his voice dropped. "She had no heart, no soul."

Jessie hesitated, blinking in bafflement. "What are you saying?"

Jarrett reached for her, but stopped. "As I told you, Angie then became, or probably always was, the consummate socialite, and I was her arm dressing. She figured a first-year med student was pliable, and she proceeded to try to mold me into the perfect, dutiful husband. For a while I let her. I was so caught up with medicine that I let her plan our life. It was all parties, fund-raisers, social commitments, and political events. I hardly had time to practice medicine, but because of her family's position, no one noticed."

Jessie's eyebrows arched and her mouth dropped a little. "I can't believe the Jarrett Collins I knew would let that happen to him."

"Neither did I, but it happened. I think the final

blow came when I told her I thought it was time we started a family. She flat-out refused, saying that no woman should ever put her body through that kind of torture for anyone. That day I finally mustered the guts to put the brakes on the roller coaster I was riding. When I finally looked around, I couldn't find me. It scared the heck out of me. I had to get away from the disaster I'd allowed to happen."

Jessie felt breathless, and, at the same time, angry for reasons even she could not put into words. She raised her head to look into his face. "So, it *is* true. You only came to Tempest to run away from your past," she said in a raw voice.

He pulled away from her and held her at arm's length. "No, Jessie, I didn't run from my past. I ran *to it*. I knew I could never come to terms with how I had messed up so many lives if I stayed in New York. We needed a clean slate; Angie and me, both." He pulled her back into his arms. He rested his chin on her head and stroked the velvet softness of her hair. "And I also knew that the only way I could begin to pick up the pieces of my miserable existence was to go back to the point when it started to go wrong; the moment I left you. Unfortunately, by coming here to you, I began another chapter in your book. Can you forgive me for assuming you'd be happy I did?"

Jessie inhaled sharply. "Jarrett . . . I can't . . ."

"Never mind. I shouldn't have said that." He wrapped his arms tighter around her. "Don't give up on me. For the last few weeks, you're all that's kept me sane and happy."

"Do you mean that now that everything's out in the open, you don't need me anymore?"

Jarrett sighed. "No. It means I still feel messed up.

But I swear, I'll get it right if you just give me some time."

In every relationship there comes a time when a decision has to be made. Jessie thought about all the years of misery he suffered. She thought about the house he built and the hope that had spawned such a task. And she thought it was time she began to believe in him too.

Jessie looked up into his eyes, taking in the man she'd come to love again, and wondering what would happen if she said it out loud now. Instead, she just shrugged. "I suppose I can wait a day or two more."

"It gets worse," Jarrett said in a muted tone. "The Ethics Committee is meeting on Monday, and I'm afraid I'm on the agenda. It seems not everyone is happy that I'm here. The Committee might . . ."

Jessie pressed her fingertips to his lips to stop the words. "I know about the hearing. If we have to face some things . . . some people, some talk, we'll work it out together."

"Can you ever forgive me for leaving you when I did?" Jarrett asked in a raw, hushed tone.

Jessie heard the pain in his voice. "I think it's time to put aside the past and all the pain that goes with it."

Jarrett held her tighter and turned over her words in his mind. If they did let go of the past, all of it, then maybe their love could carry them through what lay ahead. But would that fragile rekindled love be strong enough to buffer them against what was coming? He could only hope that it would.

"Jessie," he whispered into her hair right before he kissed its softness.

She moved against him, nestling closer. "Yes?"

He closed his eyes. "If we let go, are you sure we'll still be able to reach out and find each other?"

She looked up at him and sighed. "I surely hope so."

Chapter Eleven

J essie arranged to meet Jarrett at the coffee shop on the first floor at ten A.M. on Monday morning, after he got his car from the parking lot of McKay's. They had spent the weekend talking and preparing for the hearing as best they could, barely going out at all. He slept on the couch; she learned to eat the breakfasts he made for her.

As soon as she saw him, she could tell that something was troubling him. He was sitting uncharacteristically alone at a table near the back. She paid for her coffee and joined him.

"Maybe you should stay away," he said, finishing the last of his black coffee and crushing the Styrofoam cup in his hand.

"Why?" she asked, sliding into a chair opposite him.

Jarrett looked around the room, absorbing the cold stares of some of the occupants and quick look-aways from others. "It seems that no one wants to acknowledge the tainted doctor this morning."

In the short time she had been in the room, Jessie could already feel sharp eyes on her. "It doesn't take long for the grapevine to do its worst, Jarrett." She opened one of the small packets of sweetener, dumped it into her coffee, and mixed it with a plastic stirrer.

"I feel like everyone is taking bets on the outcome of the committee hearing," Jarrett said.

"Taking sides is more like it," she corrected. "In Tempest, everyone has an opinion."

He took her hand and massaged her knuckles with his thumb. "I have no right to do this to you, Jessie." He looked at her with sad eyes. "I'm so sorry, honey."

"Exactly what do you think you're doing to me?"

A slight quaver came into his voice. "I feel like I'm asking you choose between me and everyone else in a town you love, a town that's been your home and your haven while I was out trying to find myself."

"What are you saying, Jarrett?" Her mind suddenly blew wide open. "Are you sorry you came here for me?"

She saw hesitation in his hawklike eyes, and a terrible tenseness came into her body when he did not answer. The abrupt change in his mood from the weekend began to worry her, but before she could speak again, a loud commotion from the area near the cashier attracted their attention.

"There they are," Peggy said, loud enough for everyone in the room to hear. "The lovebirds did come up for air after all."

Jessie forced a smile as Peggy approached. "Here comes trouble," she said under her breath.

Peggy ignored the comment and settled herself on

a chair beside Jarrett. "So, when did you get your car? As of last night about eleven, it was still in the parking lot at McKay's."

"You checked?" Jarrett asked, raising his eyebrows.

"Peggy checks on everything," Jessie muttered.

"Maybe it just wouldn't start," Jarrett said. When Peggy gave him a smug grin as she stirred her coffee, he thought about giving her a quick lecture on where her nose belonged, but Dr. Silberberg stepped inside the doorway and signaled to him. He raised his hand to acknowledge and rose. "I'd love to stay and discuss the details of my life with you, Peggy, but if you'll excuse me, I have an important appointment."

Peggy rested her elbow on the table and set her chin in her hand. She glanced to Silberberg and then back to Jarrett. "So I hear."

Jessie shot Peggy a cold stare as Jarrett leaned down and gave her a light kiss on the cheek. "Wish me luck," he said.

Jessie smiled, hoping she looked more confident than she felt. "You know I do."

As he walked away, Peggy shook her finger at Jessie. "So it's true then."

"What's true?"

"You and Dr. Collins are a hot couple."

Jessie took a deep breath. "Whatever we are is none of your business, Peggy. None of anyone's for that matter."

"Quick to defend. That says something," Peggy replied coyly.

"And what would that be?" Jessie grappled with the urge to toss the rest of her coffee in Peggy's lap.

"To me, it says that you know whatever it is he's been hiding from the rest of us, but you'd rather play the modest little innocent for the sideline spectators."

"That's ridiculous," Jessie said firmly. "He isn't hiding anything."

"If you say so," Peggy muttered with a flip of her hand.

Jessie leaned her forearms onto the table. "Listen, Peggy, you're just fueling the gossip fire by talking like this. And that benefits no one. Why don't you just leave it alone?"

"Not everyone keeps to themselves the way you do, Jessie. And besides, there were some things about Dr. Collins that just didn't add up for some of us."

"Such as?"

Peggy gave Jessie a withering glare. "Most of us are dying to get out of this town, but we can't manage to find a way to do it, so we stay and make the best of it. Then Dr. Collins comes onto the scene. He's handsome, he's brilliant, and we ask ourselves the big question—why in the world would someone like him come here to Smalltown, USA, when he had his fingers on the pulse of the world in New York. Answer that one, if you dare."

"If the 'we' you're talking about are the vipers behind the nurses' station on four east," Jessie shot back at her, "you can tell them from me that it's because he's allergic to neon lights."

Peggy was not about to be put in her place. "I figured he has some skeletons in his closet. I can live with that. A little excitement, some intrigue just might shake up this place and make it interesting for a change. But then what does he do? He hooks up with a homebody pencil pusher instead of a . . ."

"Nurse with a bad reputation?" Jessie finished the sentence and glared at her with burning, reproachful eyes. "You've had your eye on him since he came to

Tempest. Maybe he just isn't buying what you're trying to sell."

Stung, Peggy slapped down her trump card. "Or
maybe the handsome doctor came out here because he
got his nice white lab coat a little dirty in the big city
and he wanted to hide out in a white-bread town with
an old pair of comfortable shoes that he remembered
was in the back of his closet."

Jessie sprang to her feet. "How dare you say something like that!"

Unwilling to be outdone, Peggy stood with her.
"Because whether you want to admit it or not, it just
might be true. If Dr. Collins has been less than honest
on his resume, people here need to know about it."

Jessie felt her face burn with anger. How she had
managed to keep her composure this long, she wasn't
sure. She knew she'd have to be careful of what she
said next because by the number of faces turned in her
direction, it was going to be all over the hospital by
the time she reached her desk in finance.

"Peggy, you're way out of line on this one. You're
just spreading vicious gossip and helping to ruin a
man's reputation. Try the truth once in a while. It's
very liberating."

"And I suppose you know the truth."

Jessie glared back at her. "Jarrett and I have known
each other for a long time, since we were children.
We're close, very close. We confide in each other and
we trust each other. So, yes, I do know the truth."

Peggy put her hands on her hips, a skeptical scowl
curling her lips. "Even if the truth is that he only married for money and to ensure that he graduated med
school and had a solid place in the community?"

A collective gasp filled the air along with her words.

Jessie looked around the room. Everyone in the coffee shop was staring at her, waiting to hear what she was going to say. She looked each one of them in the eye before speaking.

"I can't believe any of you. Most of you have worked side by side with Dr. Collins, and you know the extent of his ability and dedication. But instead of concerning yourself with the fine work he's done since he arrived, you'd rather listen to the trash Peggy's spreading. You're all waiting to turn him upside down to see if any smut falls out of his pockets." The anger blazed inside her and she stopped to discipline her voice and maintain control. "Well, I'm sorry to disappoint you, but there is none." Dead silence hung in the room as she picked up her purse and strode to the door where she spun back around. "You know, Peggy, I'm glad we had this little talk," she said in a clear voice. Glaring at Peggy one last time, Jessie turned and left the room.

Jessie shoved the pencil into the sharpener so hard that she snapped it in half. It had been over four hours since the hearing started, with no word from Jarrett.

She made another attempt to get a point on the pencil, and looked at her watch. It was already nearly two. Why hadn't she heard from him yet? She didn't even take a lunch break waiting for his call. Where was he and what was happening?

"Any word?"

Jessie looked up and felt herself relax at the sight of a friendly face. She shook her head. "Not yet."

"How are you holding up?" Ann asked, stopping just inside the doorway, waiting to see if Jessie was up for some company.

"A lot like this pencil." Jessie held up the two-inch

remnant. "Fading fast. This was fresh out of the box ten seconds ago."

Ann crossed her arms in front of her and leaned onto the door frame. "I see you haven't lost your sense of humor yet."

"I hope not. After what happened in the coffee shop, I'm going to need it when I run into Peggy again." She grimaced. "What a mess I've made."

"So fix it if you don't like the way things are turning out."

"How?"

"Begin by asking yourself what you really want."

Jessie didn't hesitate. "I want to be happy. I want Jarrett to be happy." She became suddenly serious. "And I want us to be happy together. I love him, Ann."

Ann nodded. "I guessed that. But does he know?"

Terrible regret assailed Jessie. "I'm not sure. I think so. I wanted to tell him; I really did. He gave me plenty of opportunities, but it always seemed like something got in the way."

"Just like idle talk. It gets in the way of the truth every time."

"I just wanted everything to be perfect," Jessie replied in a low, tormented voice.

Ann shook her head. "You know better than that, Jess. Things will never be perfect. You tell a man you love him when you decide that you love him. That's what makes it perfect."

Jessie's shoulders slumped. "I decided I loved him a long time ago. But maybe now it's too late."

"It's never too late." Ann smiled. "Tell him, Jessie. Before the committee passes its sentence on his career so if it turns out bad, he doesn't think you're only feeling sorry for him. He needs to hear it now."

Jessie tilted her head in a nod. "You know, Ann,

you're the only person I've talked to today who has made any sense."

"That's because I'm one of the few people in Tempest who lets all the chitchat around here go in one ear and out the other." She tapped her temple with her forefinger. "Doesn't get a chance to warp the brain cells that way." With a toss of her head she motioned to Gordon's office. "Where's the bear?"

"He got a call on his private line a few minutes ago and rushed out of here."

"Then put on the answering machine and go," Ann said. "I think you might be just what the doctor ordered."

Jarrett chased the two aspirin down his throat with a lengthy drink from the water fountain in the hall. It had been a long morning. He looked at his watch. It was past two. Morning had been over hours ago. If his head weren't pounding so much, he'd probably be hungry.

But right now he was more concerned about Jessie than about himself. She must be going crazy with worry. He walked to the house phone to call her, but decided against it even as he dialed her extension. He hung up before it rang.

He couldn't tell her anything yet. The questioning had been going around in circles for hours. There'd been a lot of hinting, a lot of innuendo, but nothing more. And the stoic faces of the seven members of the ethics panel gave him no clue as to what they might be thinking.

He shut his eyes, pinching the bridge of his nose with his forefingers. He had hoped to put his mistakes behind him when he came to Tempest for a fresh start, but apparently it was not meant to be.

And now Jessie was being drawn into the maelstrom by association. He was beginning to think he should have never come back into her life.

He checked the time once more. The ten-minute recess was nearly over. He began walking back to the conference room, when a set of heavy footsteps behind him made him turn around. It was Gordon Burrows.

"Gordon, what are you doing here?" Jarrett asked.

"Collins, I'm surprised to see you." Gordon tugged on the lapels of his gray suit and adjusted his tie. "I got a call that the committee wanted to see me. I assumed they were through with you."

Jarrett pulled his eyebrows together in a frown. "Apparently not. I'm due back in shortly."

Gordon cleared his throat. "This is rather awkward, Collins."

Jarrett nodded. "For both of us."

Gordon shifted from foot to foot like a nervous puppy. His voice cracked with uneasiness when he spoke again. "I think you should know that Pritch wants to ask me a few questions about your relationship with Miss O'Brien, and whether or not I feel it affects the department."

"Why?"

Gordon shrugged. "Who knows why Pritch does anything she does?"

"Jessie has nothing to do with what happened in New York."

"I know that." He motioned toward the conference room. "But Jessie does have a lot to do with what happens in the finance department in this hospital. Plus, she's in line for my job at the end of the year."

Jarrett strode away from him and ran a hand through his hair. "This is insane. One has nothing to do with the other." He walked back to Gordon. "Can they do this? Can they drag her into my mess and take away everything she's worked for?"

Gordon gave him a grudging nod. "This is their hospital in a matter of speaking. Most of the members of the committee are also trustees. They have the right to ask questions if they choose to do so."

"Apparently they're planning to do just that."

"They do sign the checks, in a manner of speaking."

Jarrett reached out and put his hand on Gordon's shoulder. "What are you going to tell them?"

Burrows looked from Jarrett's hand to his face. "The only thing I can, Dr. Collins. The truth as I see it."

Gordon had just entered the conference room when Jarrett saw Jessie step from the elevator. In a few steps she was in his arms.

"I had to see you, Jarrett. I was going crazy in my office imagining all sorts of ridiculous things. Are you all right? Is it over?" She rested her head on his chest.

Jarrett was still numb from his conversation with Gordon. He took her by the arms and held her away from him. "You shouldn't be here, Jessie."

Jarrett's words were stone cold, and she felt panic move into the pit of her stomach as she gazed at the distress on his face. "Something's wrong," she said, looking over his shoulder at the imposing oak door. "What is it?"

"Nothing. You should just go."

The tone of his voice sounded odd to her, but she went on. "You don't have to tell me now. After the hearing is through, you can come over and—"

"I'm not coming over."

Jessie eyes grew wide. "But why? What's happened?"

He shook his head miserably in a gesture of regret. "I was wrong to come to Tempest. I don't belong here."

Jessie gripped his arm, the shock of what she had just heard bringing the sting of tears to her eyes. "You're not thinking about leaving, are you?"

He glanced away to steel himself against the look he saw on her face. "I may have to."

"Then I'll go with you," she said in a pleading tone. "No."

The word drove a knife into her heart. She dropped her hand. "You can't mean that. Have I done something—"

He reached out and touched her arm. "No. I have."

She tried to move to him, but he held her back. "Whatever it is, we can work it out."

He shook his head, not trusting himself to speak.

"You've giving up, then? On your career here? On us?"

He looked at the pain he had put in her eyes and nearly gave in to the impulse to take her back in his arms and kiss it away. He had just sat through four hours of inane questions about his life in New York, and saw firsthand how easily the most innocent of comments got twisted into inaccuracies. He was not about to let the committee drag Jessie's personal life onto the table to dissect just to satisfy morbid curiosity and misguided concern. He had to protect her, and there was only one way he could do it. He was going to have to separate himself from her again. But this time it wouldn't be to save his career, but to save hers.

She put her hand on his arm when he did not answer. "Jarrett, please. Answer me. Are you giving up?"

"I have to go back in," he said, turning toward the

door, afraid if he looked into her eyes he would void the decision he had just made.

She stepped around him and stood between him and the door. "Don't do this, Jarrett. I love you. We'll leave together. We'll make a life somewhere else."

He raised a hand and touched her cheek. He couldn't let her throw her life away for him. This was her world, her home. Here she had a life and a career. She might be willing to leave it all for him, but he knew that she'd come to regret that decision. As the years went by, she'd come to hate him for making it.

He moved her gently aside and put his hand on the doorknob. "They're waiting for me."

She grabbed onto his arm. "I won't let you do this. You can't just come back into my life after ten years, stay for a few weeks, and then walk back out again without even so much as a thought about what it would do to me."

"I am thinking about that. Maybe for the first time since I came here." He looked at her hand and watched the knuckles turn white.

She lifted her chin and felt her lip begin to tremble. "Then I want to go in there with you."

"You can't. It's a closed meeting protected by the Sunshine Law." His voice was steady, his mouth dry. He removed her hand from his arm. "It's better this way."

"Better for whom?"

He didn't answer and started to turn the doorknob.

"Wait," she cried, struggling to find the right words to keep him from doing whatever it was that he thought he had to do in that room. But none came to her mind.

He was going to leave her.

Again.

And there was nothing she'd be able to do about it. Again.

Slowly, her gaze locked with his and she stepped out of his way.

He looked deep into her eyes and, for a moment, thought about taking her in his arms one last time. But instead, he pushed open the heavy door and stepped inside the conference room.

And, once again, stepped out of her life.

Chapter Twelve

"Dr. Collins has resigned from the staff."

"What did you say?" Jessie stopped staring at the top of her desk and snapped her head up in disbelief.

"That's what I heard," Ann said, walking into Jessie's office from the hall. "They say he up and quit." She slipped into a chair opposite Jessie. "Why in the world do you suppose he would do something like that?"

Jessie was still reeling from her conversation with him earlier. She could hardly speak. "I don't know."

"Sure you do. You said he tells you everything."

Jessie's fingers tensed in her lap. "The last thing he told me was that he didn't want to see me anymore."

"You're kidding."

"Do I look like I'm kidding?"

Ann's voice stalled. Jessie's eyes were full of tears; her face was set, jaw tense, body tight. "No. It doesn't look like you are." She pulled her brows together in a challenge. "Are you going to let him get away with it?"

Jessie stared at her. "What is that supposed to mean?"

"The man came here to get you and you're letting him leave without being got." Ann threw up her hands. "Some ending to that romantic fairy tale."

"This isn't a fairy tale. It's real life. Sometimes people don't end up happily ever after."

"Especially if neither one of them wants to fight."

Jessie set her jaw. "I tried to change his mind."

Ann leaned back. "You know what I think?"

"No, but I'm sure you're going to tell me."

"I think whatever he's doing, he's doing it for you."

Jessie stared at Ann in astonishment. "What on earth do you mean?"

Ann leaned her elbows on the desk and laced her fingers together before setting her chin on the bridge they made. "With the stories going around about him, I think he's trying to protect your reputation and your career by taking himself out of the equation before any dirt spills over onto you."

Jessie waved off the theory. "That's ridiculous."

Ann pulled her mouth into a rosette. "Not so ridiculous for someone in love. In fact, I find it rather romantic, if not a bit overdramatic."

"Romantic? You think so?"

"Yep. And if you're smart, and I know that you are, you'll finally listen to a little idle talk." She cocked a thumb in her direction. "Mine."

Jessie paused. "Do I have a choice?"

Ann shook her head. "Nope. You two belong together. Anyone can tell that. It's in his eyes when he sees you. And . . ." She reached over and lifted Jessie's chin with her fingertip. "Say his name."

"What?"

"Humor me. Say his name."

"Jarrett."

"Just as I thought. The same thing comes into your eyes when he gets inside your head." Ann sat back. "The soul is mirrored in the eyes, Jess, and your eyes say that you love him."

"That may be true, but it can't work, Ann. Not here."

Ann waved her off with the swipe of one hand through the air. "Nonsense. It works where it works. Here. There. Anywhere, as long as you want it to. You told me yourself, you knew you were supposed to be together ever since you walked down the aisle about twenty years ago in that wedding."

Jessie's mouth curved into a smile. "I did tell you that, didn't I?"

Ann stood up. "All you have to do is go to him. He thinks he's doing the right thing, so it's up to you to tell him that he's not. Go get him and bring him back, and the fourth floor be damned."

Jessie sat at the light on Seventh Street and drummed her fingertips on the top of the steering wheel. She had looked for Jarrett all over the hospital with no luck. No one had seen him and no one knew where he was.

She stared up at the red light. "Hurry up. Hurry up."

She was about four blocks from his apartment. One left turn and she'd be there. If he wasn't home, she'd wait outside until he showed up. Ann was right. It was time for her to take charge. Jarrett had left her once and she did nothing about it. This time she was going to fight.

The light changed to green about the same time the

pager she had put on the dashboard went off. After moving through the intersection Jessie eased her car to the shoulder of the road and hit the button and saw the code used for a squad call.

She looked into the rearview mirror. No one was coming. She stepped on the gas and made a U-turn.

She was back at the intersection. One way was Jarrett, the other way, someone who needed her help. She took deep breath, turned the wheel hard, and sped toward the squad building.

Mrs. Coleman. The call was for Mrs. Coleman. That's all Jessie could think as she drove the ambulance toward the hospital.

"Jessie, ETA, please!" Matt shouted from the back of the ambulance as he rhythmically compressed Martha's chest while another attendant ventilated her with the blue ambi-bag delivering life-giving oxygen.

"Five minutes, Matt," Jessie shouted back. "How's she doing?"

"Not good, Jess."

Five minutes, Jessie repeated in her mind. Five minutes and Martha would have all the help she needed.

But as she turned the corner her eyes widened and she slammed on the brakes. The ambulance skidded to a stop. The road was closed for construction work.

"Jessie," Matt hollered, kicking back the equipment that was propelled forward while still managing to maintain his rhythm on Mrs. Coleman's chest, "that's not going to help her one bit."

"Sorry." Jessie jerked the ambulance into reverse and backed around the corner. "Eighteenth Street is blocked off. I'll have to go down Mercer, then back around to pick it up on the other side." As she spoke, an icy fear twisted itself around her heart. She should have remembered about the construction. This mistake was going to cost Mrs. Coleman another five minutes at least. "Everything all right back there?" she called out, hoping.

"Sure, Jessie," Matt answered. "It'll be okay."

While Jessie frantically urged the ambulance back on course, Matt looked up from his desperate fight. The young man helping him inclined his head, on his face a question that Matt knew he had to answer somehow.

Not trusting himself to speak, he pulled his mouth into a tight line and slowly shook his head.

The knock on the front door of her apartment was the only thing that prevented Jessie from breaking into another crying jag. She sniffed and wiped her nose with a tissue. "I don't feel like company right now," she called out. "Nothing personal, just go away, okay?"

"No, it's not okay. Open up."

Jarrett. She didn't want to see him right now. Her head ached. Her eyelids burned. She was barely holding herself back from dropping her head into her hands and bawling. She was hurting enough over the death of Mrs. Coleman. She didn't need anything more. "No, not tonight."

He knocked louder. "Jessie, you shouldn't be alone. Let me in."

"Why should I?" She challenged from behind the safety of the still-closed door.

"Because."

"Because why?"

"Because if you don't I'll break down this door and the neighbors will talk about you for a week."

That got to her. She yanked the door open, her tears momentarily set aside. "Since when do you care what the neighbors think?"

"I don't. It was the only way I could think of to get you to let me inside." Jessie reached out to shut the door on him, but Jarrett grabbed her arm. "I'm worried about you. Don't send me away."

Squeezing her forehead with her fingertips to stop the tears that were again stinging her eyes, she forced herself not to cry. "Jarrett, I have a lot on my mind right now."

Gently he pushed his way inside before she could close him out. "I heard about Mrs. Coleman. I'm sorry."

His words shattered the little control she had left. Her tears burst forth like a geyser. She retreated to the sofa and buried her face in her hands, sobbing uncontrollably.

Jarrett was beside her in a second. His arms went around her and he smoothed her hair with his hand. "Shh, it's going to be all right, Jess."

"Don't do that," she begged.

"I'm sorry. I complicate things for you, don't I?"

She smothered a sob with a sigh. "God, yes."

"Do you want me to leave?"

"Yes." He started to release her, so she hung on for dear life. "No."

"Jess, what can I do to help you through this?"

His voice sounded anxious, concerned, as if he were sure this was the last chance he was ever going to have to be with her. It was her undoing. "Oh Jarrett, I killed her. I forgot all about the construction on Eighteenth Street." She sobbed, stuttering through the words and trying to catch her breath between sentences. "It's my fault she's dead."

Jarrett rocked her back and forth. "No, it's not. When I heard about Mrs. Coleman, I was afraid that you were going to blame yourself so I went back to the hospital and checked. She had a massive coronary. There was too much damage." He kissed the top of her head as she rested it on his shoulder. "She was probably gone at the house. There was nothing anyone could have done to save her no matter when you got her to the hospital."

Jessie lifted her teary eyes and ran the back of one hand under her nose. "Are you sure?"

He nodded.

"But no one ever died in my ambulance before. How am I going to drive it again?" Jessie looked stricken. Her mouth quivered and she slumped against him.

He stroked her hair as he spoke. "You'll drive it because you're a professional and because people are counting on you to do your job."

Jessie sat silent for a moment. Then she sat up straight and looked at him. She tore herself from his arms and headed for the box of tissues in the kitchen.

"Why should I take advice from a coward?" she suddenly challenged.

Jarrett's chin snapped up in surprise. "Jessie?"

"You're the last person in this town who should be giving me advice about professionalism and doing a job." She wiped her eyes and blew her nose.

"I don't understand, Jess."

"I think you do, but you're too afraid to face it." Jessie began to pace the kitchen as thoughts flooded her head. It suddenly became crystal clear what she had to do. She prayed she had enough strength left to do it.

"Jessie, please, you're upset. You don't know what you're saying."

"Oh, I most certainly do. You come here after leaving me ten years ago and make pretty speeches about still loving me." She stopped, spun around, and pointed an angry finger at him from the other room. "Buddy, that tossed me for a loop. But I thought, okay, listen to the guy. So I listened and pretty soon I started to believe. Worse than that, I began to love you back. Then what happens?" She slammed a palm onto the kitchen table hard enough to send the salt shaker tumbling to the floor. "Bam. Just like before, you quit on me. Then you quit your job." She glared at him. "So how dare you come here tonight lecturing me about professionalism and loyalty? When it came down to a matter of it getting a little uncomfortable for you, you left again."

"That's not true," he answered quickly.

"Then tell me," she challenged again.

Jarrett was silent for a moment. "I didn't quit on you."

Jessie gave him a very unladylike snort and crossed her arms in front of her chest.

"I didn't quit on you," he reaffirmed. "I had to choose between you and me, and this time, I picked you."

"What do you mean—you picked me?"

He walked into the kitchen to be near her. "The committee was about to lay bare your personal life just to satisfy their curiosity. That was not going to happen if I had anything to do about it. You're much too important to me to be made the topic of conversation over hospital coffee."

"So you resigned," Jessie said slowly. She drew down her eyebrows. Ann was right, she thought.

He nodded.

"To protect my reputation."

He nodded again.

Jessie put her hands to her hips and stuck out her bottom lip. "Well, you're not getting away with it."

Jarrett's eyes grew wide. "Jessie, what on earth do you mean? I'm trying to save your—"

She cut him off with the swipe of a hand. "If anyone needs saving around here, it isn't me!"

"If you'd let me explain."

"No. You're going to listen to me for a change." She pointed to a chair and waited until he sat down. Experiencing the events of the past few days was like awakening from a long sleep. She finally knew what had to be done, what had to be said. "If Mrs. Coleman's death teaches me anything today," she stopped and inhaled deeply to quell another bout of grief that stabbed at her, "it'll be that there are some things we simply have no control over and some things we can control."

Jarrett saw her chest heave in a sigh and started to come to her. "Jessie, are you all right?"

She raised a hand to stop him. If he touched her again, she would be too distracted to continue. She had to finish while everything was fresh in her mind. He nodded and sat back down.

She ignored the trembling in her limbs and continued. "What do you intend to do with the rest of your life now that you've resigned from the hospital?"

Jarrett's eyebrows rose in a quizzing expression. "I'm not sure yet. I only resigned from my position as Chief of Emergency Medicine."

Jessie clapped her hands together. "Good. That means you still have your affiliation, so you can still practice medicine in Tempest at Midwest Medical."

Jarrett raised his hands. "You're losing me."

She gave him a cocked hip pose. "Not this time.

Quite the contrary, I'm saving your sorry butt. If you'll let me continue, that is."

He swept a hand in the air. "By all means. I'm intrigued."

"You're a good man, Jarrett. You're honorable, intelligent, hard-working, and passionate about what you do, both in and out of the hospital." She paused, the faint beginnings of an affectionate smile curling her lips upward. "Besides, you're much too cute to waste."

As the atmosphere in the room began to warm with Jessie's smile, Jarrett began to let himself relax. "Thanks, I think."

She continued, waving her hands around in the air. "But you have no direction. You're wandering through life without grabbing onto it, and so am I."

"How do you mean?"

Once again, just like all those years earlier, Jessie knew the next few minutes were again going to be some of the most important ones in her life. As she walked toward him, she quickly pulled all her thoughts together. "You take on too much and you won't let anyone help you."

"Not true," he countered.

" 'Fraid so. Look at the pattern. You left me because you thought you were doing the right thing for both of us, but you never asked me if that was what I wanted."

"I guess I did," he conceded.

"Then, without so much as a whimper, you let yourself get talked into getting married to a woman who needed a husband for social climbing. Quite foolish."

"I guess I'm easily distracted."

"Apparently." She put a finger to his lips. "Think about this before you answer. Do you love me, Jarrett Collins?"

"I think I always have."

"Will you love me forever?"

He smiled slowly, remembering a time he should have answered that question as confidently as he was going to answer it now.

"Forever."

"Promise. No matter what?"

Jarrett frowned. "What's wrong?"

"It's a scary world out there, and we have to face it together. You don't seem to like anyone helping you with decisions. That's what's wrong. Just like it was wrong of me to allow myself to believe that if someone died in my ambulance, it was my fault. I'm going to need someone to lean on when I fall, and so are you. I need someone who will trust me with the bad as well as the good. Can you do that, Jarrett?"

When she fell? That probably was what did it. If anyone was going to catch Jessie when she fell, it was going to be him. And if she was willing to be there for him, it was all he was ever going to need.

He suddenly began to believe in himself again. He drew her close and touched his forehead to hers. "What can we do to fix this distraction problem I seem to have developed over the years?" As soon as he said the words, he held his breath, afraid he had asked too much.

She moved back, not a lot, just enough to look into his eyes. "We can take charge of our lives. Both of us. You left me once and I didn't lift one finger to stop you. But not this time. You came here looking for me. Well, here I am. I love you, Jarrett Collins. I promised myself a long time ago that I was going to marry you and I have every intention of keeping that promise."

He grinned at her. "Are you proposing?"

"Are you accepting?"

Jarrett shifted his gaze to the ceiling. "Let me think about it."

Jessie poked him in the ribs. "You aren't getting a third chance."

"Ouch. Okay, you don't have to torture me. I'll marry you."

"But there is a condition attached," she said.

"And that would be?"

"We stay here. In Tempest. No more running away. We build the house we planned to build all those years ago and fill it with children." She felt a warm glow course through her. "But this time, we do it together."

Jarrett smiled broadly. "Best offer I've had in about ten years."

"Then you're staying?"

His smile grew even wider. "Why not? I hear that Tempest needs a pediatrician, and I need a job."

Jessie raised her eyebrows. "Listening to idle talk, Doctor?"

"Nope. Facts." Jarrett slid an arm around her neck. "And another fact I should have listened to a long time ago was my heart telling me to never let you go."

She smiled. "As I said, sometimes you just need a little help."

Any response she may have gotten from Jarrett was lost in his kiss.

Epilogue

This time Jarrett stood in the front vestibule of St. John's Church waiting for Jessie, not waiting with her in the back. He stuck his finger inside the collar of the starched white tuxedo shirt and tried to stretch it away from his throat.

"A little nervous about walking out there in front of all those people?" Steve Silberberg asked, patting his pants pockets, making sure he had the rings.

"Not really." Jarrett walked to the vestibule door and looked out. He smiled, remembering. "We've done this once before already."

Steve looked over Jarrett's shoulder. "Third row from the back. Isn't that Pritch Stewart? After what happened, I'm surprised you would invite her."

Pitch nodded perfunctorily when Jarrett caught her eye. "We didn't. I guess this is her way of telling me that all is forgiven."

"The lady doesn't like to lose. When the Ethics

Committee voted to ask you to reconsider your resignation, I thought she was going to faint dead away."

Jarrett grinned. "If she had, I would have been more than willing to administer the CPR."

"That would have killed her for sure." Steve saw Jarrett's grin threaten to widen with the comment. "Decorum, Doctor. You're about to be wed. And that's no laughing matter."

"Sorry," Jarrett said, feigning a cough.

Steve glanced at his watch. "You have about five minutes of freedom left. You can still duck out the back."

Jarrett shook his head. "Not this time. No more running for me."

He looked out again and saw Jessie's Aunt Judy and Grandma Ginger being escorted to their seats. He saw Judy nudge Ginger and gesture in his direction. He gave them a small wink and they blew him a kiss in return. In another minute, Jessie's mother was seated, and the music began.

"Okay, it's time," Steve said. "Are you ready to walk the last mile of freedom?"

"I've been ready for years," Jarrett said. "Let's go."

When they took their places in front of the minister, the guests rose to watch the bride walk down the aisle on the arm of her father. But Jarrett didn't hear the music or see anyone in the pews. All he saw was Jessie.

She was wearing the antique wedding gown both her grandmother and her mother had worn when they had gotten married in this very church. It was at the moment their eyes locked that he knew beyond a shadow of a doubt they had been drawn to this moment by forces beyond their control. Overcoming time and circumstances, they had somehow succeeded in finding the path back to each other's hearts.

As Jessie came closer, Jarrett saw Jessie lower her eyes to her bouquet and his gaze followed. He grinned. There, sitting in the center, amid the pink roses, tinted carnations, and sprigs of baby's breath, was the baseball card she had taken from him so long ago.

After her father kissed her on the cheek and put her hand into Jarrett's, Jessie reached into her flowers and held out the card. "I told you that you would get this back when you earned it," she whispered.

Jarrett saw the same depth to her smile as there had been when she took the card from him all those years earlier.

"You can have it back now," she said.

His mouth curled with tenderness. He took the card and tucked it inside the cummerbund at his waist. Then he took her hand again and promised to never let it go.

Before family and friends, Jessie and Jarrett reaffirmed the undeniable love they held for each other. It flamed and intensified in the promises they made as their wedding vows were finally spoken.

To love . . . to cherish . . . from this day forward . . . for all the days of their lives.